Saving Grace

Amy R. Anguish

Scrivenings
PRESS
Quench your thirst for story.
www.ScriveningsPress.com

Published by Scrivenings Press LLC
15 Lucky Lane
Morrilton, Arkansas 72110
https://ScriveningsPress.com

Printed in the United States of America

Paperback ISBN 978-1-64917-001-9

eBook ISBN 978-1-64917-064-4

Library of Congress Control Number: 2020946113

Cover by Linda Fulkerson, bookmarketinggraphics.com

The creativity has always been inside me, but several people in particular saw the potential in my stories and helped me polish my craft to truly let it shine. I'd like to dedicate this novel to Wilburta Arrowood and Sandi Rog, two fellow authors who took me under their wings and taught me to fly.

You have both been a huge blessing in my life and I thank God for you!

PROLOGUE

*S*he couldn't breathe.

Ringing filled her ears.

Michelle Wilson forced her eyelids open, one at a time. Dust floated in the air, leftover from the airbag deploying only moments earlier. Her car no longer moved, but somewhere a horn blared on and on.

Drawing a tentative breath, she squinted at her surroundings. Her head spun even though the vehicle was still. She fumbled for her purse. Where had it landed? She undid her seatbelt and pushed the deflated airbag out of the way. With fumbling fingers, she grabbed the bag from the floorboard and pulled her cellphone out.

"911, what's your emergency?"

"I've been in a wreck."

"Okay, ma'am. Are you injured? Can you tell me your location?"

Michelle looked around until she spotted the street sign. Her car must have spun around during the wreck. "Windom and Lancaster, Little Rock."

"Was anyone else hurt?"

"There was another car. I'm not really sure what happened."

"Can you see the other car?"

"Umm ..." Michelle glanced around but didn't see it. As she pulled on the door handle, a sharp pain shot up her arm. Blood pounded in her ears. She slowly released a breath through clenched teeth, eased the door open, then stood on shaky legs.

"Ma'am, are you okay?" The 911 operator's voice sounded in her ear, bringing her focus back to the task at hand.

"I'm hurt, but I need to find the other vehicle." There it was. A pickup truck lay on its side about twenty feet away, one of the rear wheels still spinning. "It looks like it's flipped over a couple of times. I can't see any movement from inside."

"The police are just a few blocks away. Stay still, and they'll be there in just a couple of minutes, okay?"

Michelle nodded, then realized the girl couldn't see her. "Okay."

Lowering herself slowly to the ground, she put her head on her knees to stop the dizziness. Even with her eyes closed, the world spun out of control. The warm April evening had started so well, but now seemed as cold as the late-season snow they'd had back in March.

Flashing lights and a siren blast soon filled the area.

Before she could protest, someone lifted her from where she'd slumped against the side of her car and placed her on a stretcher.

"The other car—"

"We're helping them, too, miss. Please be still so we can make sure you're okay."

Michelle turned her head to see the other vehicle. Were they all right? Across the intersection, emergency workers pulled a male driver from the pickup truck. His features were hard to make out through all the blood. Several other EMS workers rushed over to a woman lying in the street in front of the vehicle. Michelle frowned. How did the woman get there?

A commotion drew her attention back to the man. He'd

regained consciousness and thrashed against the restraints of his stretcher.

"My wife. Leah!" He screamed as they pushed him toward the other ambulance. "You've got to help my wife. Our baby!"

"Sir, are you saying there's a baby still in the truck?"

"No." The man shook his head. "She's pregnant. In labor. We were about to have a baby!"

An icy wave rolled down Michelle's spine. The woman still hadn't moved. *Please, God, no.* If the woman was dead, the baby might also be dead. Could this previously perfect night possibly get worse?

They faced each other as EMS loaded them into the ambulances. The man's eyes locked with Michelle's, and it was as if a force connected them despite the distance.

"Please, save my baby." Still pleading with the ambulance driver, his gaze held hers.

Had his plea been meant for Michelle? Could he see her through all the blood dripping from his forehead? Surely not. He didn't even know Michelle. And yet—it was like a command had been given to her. She wouldn't rest until she knew that baby was safe.

The ambulance doors closed, and they moved her left wrist. Pain cut through her like a knife, straight to her head. Everything went dark.

THE NEXT DAY, Michelle stood at the window of the hospital's nursery. She looked through the glass at the little girl wrapped in a pink blanket. The name on the placard said *Grace*. The nurses told her it was the last word the baby's father said after they told him he had a little girl. Before he died. Michelle pressed her hand against the pane and leaned her head against its coolness.

Grace's eyes fluttered open and looked directly at Michelle. Michelle straightened, her breath caught somewhere deep in her lungs. The gaze was almost an exact replica of the child's father when he'd pleaded for someone to save his baby.

Well, here they were now, the only two survivors of the disastrous wreck that had stolen the lives of both Grace's parents. Even though newborns supposedly couldn't see far away, Grace's gaze never wavered for a full five minutes. It was as if God were sending Michelle a sign. A reinforcement of the message she'd received the night before.

She and that child were now bonded for life. Soul sisters, forged through the pain of loss with matching battle scars across their hearts. A plan formed in her mind that would maintain that link for a long time to come. Michelle had only slept a few hours, but she was energized enough to know the right thing to do. This little girl needed her. It wasn't fair to the baby to have to start her life with no one to love her.

"Which one is yours?" a man interrupted.

"That one." Michelle didn't hesitate.

He nodded. "That one's mine." He pointed to a little bundle in blue with a full head of dark hair.

"He's beautiful." Michelle glanced over at his child for a second before turning back to Grace.

"Do you get to take her home today?" He tipped up on his toes as if to get a better angle.

"I hope so." Michelle swallowed her worry. "I hope so."

CHAPTER 1

"*I* can do this." Michelle released a tension-filled breath. "It's just a car."

A glance down at the baby sleeping peacefully in the carrier looped over her arm alleviated some of the nervousness. She'd been driving for over ten years now. Michelle refused to let one little wreck—okay, big wreck—the week before keep her from driving again. Nor would this stupid cast covering her left wrist and part of her forearm. She could still wiggle her fingers.

After several deep lungsful to steady her nerves, she loaded Grace into the back seat. She ran a hand over the straps to make sure they were secure. If for no other reason than this child, she'd be the most careful driver in the world.

"Can't have you losing me too."

Michelle shook her head to clear the darkness threatening her vision. She could do this, despite what happened the last time she drove. This would be a happy day. She was headed to see her best friend again for the first time since Christmas. And he didn't even expect her to be anywhere near Cedar Springs, Arkansas. She grinned at the baby.

"Let's go introduce you to one of my favorite people in the world."

Hands on the steering wheel, she squeezed her eyes closed against the panic threatening her joy and tightening her throat. Driving was like riding a bicycle, right? It wasn't like maniac motorcyclists ran red lights at every intersection. She forced her eyelids open and started the ignition. Only a few blocks. Straightening her shoulders, she inched out of the driveway.

Ten uneventful minutes later, she pulled into the familiar parking lot and wrangled Grace's car seat out. The church building hadn't changed at all. It even smelled the same as when Michelle attended services here as a child—of books and lemon-scented cleaner.

She walked down the linoleum-floored hallway toward the kitchen. The secretary said he was back here getting things ready for a lock-in this weekend. His singing carried through the air as she neared the doorway. She tiptoed to the corner and peeked around.

Gregory Marshall pulled several folding chairs off the rack and placed them in neat rows facing one another. Probably to play fun games or for the devotional parts of Friday night. He'd always been so organized, unlike Michelle. As he lifted another stack of seats down, his muscles bulged more than she remembered in high school, though otherwise, he was much the same. And his chestnut curls were cut shorter than the mop he'd worn as a teen.

A smile stretched across her face as he continued belting out the song.

"I'll fly away, O glory. I'll fly away."

"When I die, hallelujah, by and by." She joined him at the last of the verse. "I'll fly away."

He turned, a huge grin on his face, his blue eyes twinkling. "Mickey?"

Other than her daddy, he was the only person in the world she let use her childhood nickname.

6

GREG'S HEART tripped over itself when his favorite person stepped around the corner. Michelle's brown hair hung just past her shoulders, like it had since she grew out what she always referred to as 'the bowl cut' her mom got her in second grade. Her glasses didn't hide the bruising around her blue eyes, and his heart squeezed at how much it must have hurt.

Two giant steps toward a long overdue hug, he froze. A cast covered one of her arms, and a baby carrier swung from the other. His head cocked to the side as he studied the contraption and the child in it.

"Your parents get a new foster?"

"Sort of." Michelle cast a glance at the sleeping infant. "Officially, yes. But unofficially, no."

"I don't understand."

"She's ... well, hopefully, mine."

"Yours?" All sorts of scenarios ran through his mind, most of them breaking his heart. How long had it been since he'd seen her last?

"For now." Michelle set Grace down and opened her arms for the hug he'd started a moment before.

After a short pause, he wrapped his arms around her and squeezed. She leaned into him, her head nestling perfectly under his chin. As many times as he'd dreamed of this reunion, it was even better in reality.

"You're here." Greg let her go and headed back to get more chairs. "How long?"

"Always."

Michelle bumped into his back when he stopped right in front of her.

Greg turned and cocked an eyebrow at her.

"I've been offered my dream job. I start at the *Sun* on Monday." While some people wanted to work at nationally recognized papers, have their names in bylines all over the country and world, Michelle had always dreamed of being a photojournalist for the local paper. For years she'd talked about how she'd rather be recognized among those who loved her.

"You're back for good?"

"For good."

They sat in folding chairs and just grinned at each other for a moment.

"Your mom told me you were in a wreck, and they were headed your way. I need details." Greg leaned back and folded his arms across his chest. He'd been praying and fretting for days, wondering how she was.

She breathed in and out a couple of times, obviously working up the nerve to relive her memories. "Several of my friends threw me a party the night before I was supposed to move back." She picked at a loose piece of cotton sticking out from her cast. "We stayed up late, giggling and not wanting the night to end because it was the last time we'd probably be together.

"I was tired, but I didn't live far from there, so I didn't think anything of it. Unfortunately, a few blocks from my apartment, a motorcycle blew through the intersection's red light in front of me."

He hunched forward, his elbows on his knees, soaking in every word. The urge to go hunt down the idiot who'd caused so much stress in her life had him forcing his hands not to fist. No need to upset her more.

"I swerved to make sure I didn't clip the back of his bike, but I didn't see the pickup truck headed my way. I guess they did the same thing because they swerved toward me. The truck ended up spinning and flipping. I did a one-eighty before I finally stopped. I think I may have passed out after I called 911. When they got there, I was slumped next to my car door. And I fainted again when they touched my wrist."

He leaned forward and touched her knee. "And the people in the truck?"

"Grace's parents." She glanced down at the still-sleeping

infant, a tear winding its way down her cheek. "They were actually on their way to the hospital to have her."

"Mickey." Her name came out as almost a sigh.

"Leah, Grace's mom, was unbuckled for some reason. When the truck flipped ... she flew through the window." Michelle swiped at the moisture on her face. "John, her husband—he wouldn't let the EMTs do anything to him until they'd done all they could for Leah. And because he refused treatment for so long, the internal bleeding—"

Greg wrapped his arm around her shoulders and pulled her to him. How many times had he dreamed of holding Michelle like this? But not with the reason behind it. He wouldn't wish that on anyone, especially not his best friend, who tended to be empathetic almost to a fault.

Finally, she leaned away and grabbed an old napkin from a nearby table to dab her cheeks. "It was definitely the scariest thing I've ever been through." She sniffled. "And the saddest. I mean, they were alive when we got in the ambulances but gone the next morning."

He gave her fingers a squeeze. It wasn't enough, but what else could he do?

"So much changed in such a short time." She lifted her broken arm as she spoke, never able to talk without moving her hands.

"Does your wrist hurt?" He gently touched her cast.

"Not really. It's more of a nuisance than anything. Although it may have me typing 'hunt and peck' for a while. And I haven't figured out how I'm going to use my camera yet." She drew in a deep breath.

"But nothing hurts as much as the thought that Grace will never really know her parents. I mean, I know the state is sorting things out and figuring out what all needs to stay tucked away so she can know a bit about her family in the future. But she'll never know everything about them. It's so unfair."

"And who told you life is fair?" Greg quoted the saying her dad had always teased them with when they were growing up.

"Thanks, Dad." Michelle rolled her eyes.

"So, how did you end up in charge of Grace? I mean, doesn't she have grandparents or someone who can take her?"

"No known close relatives. This poor kid was about to end up in the system. The caseworker actually said she'd have to call around to try and find a foster home on such short notice. We couldn't let that happen. Not with Mom and Dad still active through the children's home in Paragould. My parents are officially fostering her right now while the state works things out. But, I'm hoping I can adopt her."

Greg leaned back, stunned into partial breathlessness. In all the years of wishing and hoping for a reunion with Michelle, and even a closer relationship than what they'd enjoyed in the past, he'd never considered this. If she adopted the baby, would that change everything? She'd always been a go-getter, one to conquer goals and reach for dreams, no matter how far away. But if she could make this happen, would she even want a man in her life?

Grace stirred a moment in her sleep and stilled again. Michelle leaned down and brushed the side of her finger against the baby's soft skin, causing his heart to skip. Would a baby born to the two of them look like Grace?

He waged war with himself, not wanting to crush this plan, but also wary. After all, Michelle hadn't always been the responsible one of the two of them. Could she take care of a child by herself? How did he offer counsel without giving the support she expected?

"You don't think it's a good idea." She sat back up.

"I don't know. I mean, you're temporarily living with your parents. You're not sure how to work your camera with your hand in a cast. You don't even know if Grace will be available for adoption. Mickey, there's a lot to consider. You can't just make a snap decision about this like you did with so many things in high school."

"I know that. This isn't whether or not to run for class president or who I'm going to prom with. This is serious." Michelle fisted her hands in her lap. "I know we haven't talked as much as we wanted the last few years, but I have grown up some, Greg. I can make hard decisions now."

"Have you prayed about it?"

"I'm not part of your youth group. Don't beat me over the head with how to talk to God, okay? That's not why I came here today. I thought my move back would be a good surprise for you, that you'd be happy to see me again."

"I am happy you moved back. You know that." He dashed his hands through his hair.

"But?"

"But I'm worried about you. It's like you're trying to make your life harder than it has to be."

"You don't understand. I have to adopt Grace."

"Why? Make me understand." He stood and paced in front of her.

"I just have to."

A myriad of expressions floated across her face, but none stayed long enough for him to interpret. What was going on in that mind of hers?

"It's the right thing to do."

"The right thing to do?"

"I just ..." Michelle flopped her hands in her lap. "I want to make it up to her."

"Mick." He knelt in front of her. "You know it's not your fault her parents died, right?"

Michelle looked across the room, blinking back a tear. "But it's at least partly my fault."

"No." He tugged at her fingers to get her attention. "No. You didn't make Leah unbuckle her seatbelt. You didn't even know they'd be on the road. As far as I know, you didn't even know them. And I'm sure you didn't make that motorcycle fly through that red light. You only had control over you. And you did what you could to save them all. You don't have to make it up to her."

She pulled her quivering bottom lip between her teeth. "But I want to. And it just feels like this is the direction God wants me to go."

"You know I'm always here for you." He shook his head and let out a breath. "I'll never understand you, but I'm always here."

"I know." She grinned at him.

"I'll do anything I can to help." He wanted to say more, but Grace started fussing.

Her cries echoed off the empty walls of the fellowship room. Michelle quickly unbuckled the baby and lifted her carefully from the car seat. Greg had to admit he was impressed with how well she maneuvered despite the cast. She leaned down and looked through the side pocket of the diaper bag, pulling out a bottle.

"Hang on, sweetie." She crooned to Grace.

"How can I help?"

She looked up as he hovered nearby and raised an eyebrow. "Want to hold her while I fix her bottle?"

Teenagers he could handle, but a newborn? He swallowed, then nodded. How hard could it be? She gently transferred Grace into his arms and positioned his hands under the baby's head and back. Before he felt comfortable, she headed toward the kitchen with the sustenance the child obviously wanted.

"What do I do now?" Greg asked, hoping the panic trying to escape didn't show in his voice.

"Rock her a bit. I'll have this fixed in a minute."

She made it sound so simple. He cast back through memories, searching for what he'd seen others do with a crying child. Sing. He could do that—anything to get this pitiful wailing to stop.

~

WHEN MICHELLE RETURNED from the kitchen, Greg cradled Grace in the crook of his arm and swayed in rhythm to the tune of the hymn he softly sang. The little girl looked up at him with her big eyes, her face splotchy from crying, still whimpering, but not all-out fussing anymore.

Michelle's heart skipped a beat, and she stared for a moment at the picture they made together. He was a natural. She shook her head, not sure why it affected her so much to see him holding the baby she already considered hers.

"Looks like you have it under control." Michelle somehow got the words out around the lump in her throat.

He looked up and shrugged a bit.

She handed him the bottle. He fumbled at first as he situated it and the baby at the same time. Michelle reached over and positioned his hand at a better angle for fewer bubbles.

"Thanks." His breath whispered across her cheek.

Only inches separated their faces. Her heart skipped another beat, and she stepped back, pulling her fingers away from where they'd lingered on his. What was wrong with her today? This was *Greg.*

Grace sucked noisily, and both adults smiled down at her.

"Do women just automatically know what to do when a baby cries?"

"It's fairly easy to figure out when they're this age." Michelle took a step back. "They're either tired, gassy, hungry, or have a dirty diaper."

"I'm glad it wasn't the last one." Greg wrinkled his nose.

"She's not finished with the bottle yet."

His head jerked up, and she laughed. They sat side-by-side in the chairs again, each lost in their own thoughts, wrapped in comfortable silence.

"The memorial service for her parents is in Little Rock on Saturday. I think I should take her." Michelle picked at another spot on her cast that hadn't glued down smoothly.

"By yourself?" Greg shot her a sideways glance.

"Know of a better way?"

"I'll go with you."

"It's not like I haven't driven back and forth to Little Rock a hundred times over the last few years. I think I can handle it. Cedar Springs is less than two hours from there."

"But you weren't all bruised up and wearing a cast, not to mention having a baby to worry about. What if she starts crying while you're on the highway?"

"Then, I'll find a place to pull over so I can fix whatever's wrong." Michelle shrugged. "And the bruises and cast won't slow me down that much."

He studied her face.

"How bad does it really look? I've been avoiding looking at myself in detail in the mirror. Just enough of a glance to do a ponytail and make sure my teeth are brushed."

"It's pretty gruesome." He tenderly reached over and traced her right eye. "It's a shame it's not Halloween. A lot of the kids would love to have that kind of face for their costume."

She stuck her tongue out at him. "Bet they wouldn't want the achiness that came with it. Who knew a seatbelt and airbag could hurt so much?"

"Better to have bruises and aches than not to have worn the seatbelt."

She sighed. "Like Leah."

"Sorry. I wasn't even thinking about that."

"No." Michelle shook her head. "I just can't get it off my mind. It's definitely made me more careful about everyone buckling up."

Grace finished her bottle. Michelle showed Greg how to prop her up and pat her back until the burp came—just like her mother had shown her only days before. They loaded Grace back into the carrier and stood.

"So, what time do I need to pick you up on Saturday?"

"Seriously, you don't have to do this. You'll be dead on your feet after being at the lock-in all night."

"Then, I'll let you drive if I get sleepy. I really don't want you to go alone, Mickey. Please."

Michelle huffed. "Fine."

"You're just afraid of how much I'll find out since we'll have all that time in the car to catch up."

"Ha." Michelle laughed. "Or not. Probably you have more to tell than I do."

"You know things here don't ever change."

"I've missed small-town life."

"It's good to have you back." He pulled her into another hug.

"It's good to be back." She leaned into his solid frame for an extra moment. Even though she'd been back in Cedar Springs for a couple of days, this was the first time she really felt like she was home.

"I'm preaching Sunday." Greg helped her loop the diaper bag over her shoulder. "Les and Patty are headed to Oklahoma to see their granddaughter perform in a play at her college."

"Wow. Was that a warning?" Michelle poked him in the arm.

"Ouch. You used to think it was cool when I preached."

"I still do. You're a good speaker. Even if you do sermonize a bit too much out of the pulpit sometimes."

"Got to practice, ya know?"

"You'll have a full weekend." She shook her head.

"I'll just sleep all day Monday. It'll be fine." He took the carrier from her. "I've got this."

She followed him down the hallway, not quite sure what to make of the visit. Greg was still the same, but things hadn't seemed the same between them. Maybe she was imagining things. Probably, it was just lack of sleep.

"I'll see you Saturday." Greg pulled her into one more hug after she situated everything in the back of the car.

"See you then." As much as she'd been looking forward to having him back in her life, she was almost nervous about him joining her.

CHAPTER 2

*F*riday morning, Michelle opened the front door to a woman in a neat pantsuit.

"Michelle?" The woman thrust her hand out in a brisk, business-like manner. "I'm Diane, Grace's caseworker."

"Yes. We're expecting you." Michelle squeezed Diane's fingers. This was the woman who could make or break Michelle's plans. "Come on in."

Hopefully, the classic style of the living room would meet with approval. The furniture hadn't been updated in a while, but it was clean and comfortable. Besides, if Michelle had her way, she and Grace wouldn't be living here too long before they could get settled in their own place.

Mom and Dad sat on the couch in the living room, Grace between them. Dad had taken off the rest of the week to help get everything worked out. Good thing, too. When she'd decided to move back a week before her new job started at the newspaper office, she hadn't counted on the days flying by in the madness that ensued after her wreck. Michelle perched on the edge of a rocking chair across from Diane, who'd chosen the loveseat.

"First and foremost, let me just say that it's very honorable, what you are proposing to do." Diane smiled at everyone in turn.

Michelle released a breath she hadn't even realized she was holding. That had to be a good start, right?

"We've been madly scrambling the last few days to learn more about this situation. As far as we can tell, John and Leah didn't have any other living family. We're still looking into it to make sure, but their parents had all passed on, and they were only children themselves." She flipped through a manilla file in her lap.

"We've been able to find their wills, and discovered they hadn't set up specific guardians. They did leave guidelines they want the trustee of their wills to uphold. Right now, we're still trying to track this guy down. From what we can tell, they had moved to Little Rock within the last month, and this man lives in their old hometown. Until we can locate him and work out the details of their estate plan, Grace will have to remain under the care of the state."

Michelle grimaced. She hated the thought of the baby being passed around until the legal system could get their act together. Evidently, her father did too.

"She's okay to remain with us as a foster, right?"

Diane nodded. "Yes. You have no idea what a relief it was to have you already in the system and able to take her in so quickly this week. Normally, when we get a baby like this, we have to hustle to find a family with room."

"God obviously put us where we were needed the other night." Mom smiled. "It's been a while since we fostered, but we always keep everything up-to-date just in case."

Diane gave a short nod. "Once we find the trustee of John's and Leah's wills, we'll know more about where we'll go from there. We'll still be researching, trying to find out if there are any other living family members or close friends who'd want to take the child in. We try to stick as closely as we can to what the parents would have wanted."

Dad placed a hand on the baby's foot. "We're more than happy to keep her until something else can be arranged."

"Perfect." Diane handed him a tablet. "If you could fill out this form, I think that's all we need today. It's just a few things we didn't get to in the whirlwind of the hospital the other day."

"No problem." Mom stood.

"And I'll keep you updated as we find things out." Diane stuck a few papers back in her bag. "She looks like she's in great hands, though."

Grace fussed, and Michelle quickly scooped her up to change her diaper. "Can you mention my thoughts while I do this?" She sent her mom a pointed look.

Mom pursed her lips but then nodded.

THAT AFTERNOON, Mom sat at the kitchen counter across from her, lemonades condensating in front of them. The side of the island still bore a mark from where Michelle and her brother had each lost scooter races—as well as a tooth or two—as kids. Michelle ran her tongue over the space now grown in slightly crooked.

Mom exchanged a glance with Dad. "So, they can't let you officially be the foster parent."

"What?" Michelle jerked her hand through the air. "Why not?"

"Because you've never been one." Dad leaned forward from his stance near the stove. "You have to pass the background checks, the home studies, et cetera. They can't just let anyone foster who wants to."

"But I would pass all those checks. You've been foster parents since I was four. I probably know as much about it as you do."

"Michelle, there are other things that stand in your way if

you really want to pursue this." Mom's fingers drummed a rhythm on the marble.

Michelle waited for the bomb to drop.

"You're not in a stable situation, yet."

"I'm not unstable." Michelle frowned.

"They want children in the foster system to be in a steady environment, usually preferring the foster parent, well, to be married. To have their own residence. One person working full-time, and both having enough time to do home visits or whatever else needs to happen."

"I'll get married eventually. I just haven't found the right guy yet."

"Yes, honey. We're not saying we want you to rush and get married. We just want you aware. It's one of the normal requirements of fostering." Her mom scooted a package of cookies nearer the center of the bar.

"What if I decided never to get married, but that I do want kids? Would I not be able to adopt, either, just because I decided I don't need a husband?"

"Not through some agencies." Dad patted her shoulder. "And you know I never wanted you to grow up and get married, Mickey. But I agree you should be married before you have kids. Children function better in a home with a mom and a dad, not just one or the other."

Michelle spun her stool around. One step forward and two steps back. How could she convince these people she wasn't just saying she wanted this—that she really did?

"The state has agreed to let your father and me be the legal foster parents while everything gets worked out. It's easier on the children's home if they don't have to deal with infants, so they pulled some strings to let us pick up where we left off several years ago with fostering for them. We'll keep Grace with us for now, and we'll figure it out as we go." Mom squeezed her shoulder as Michelle walked by to put her glass in the sink.

"Want to start looking at cars this evening?"

Dad had somehow found time to talk to the insurance company about Michelle's vehicle. She'd hear from them in the next few days, but he was pretty sure they'd total it.

"Not really." Michelle scuffed her toe against the corner of the rug that always curled up. "Thanks for all your help with it and the loan of your cars in the meantime. I know this isn't an ideal situation, but I can't handle the thought of dealing with salesmen right now."

"I understand." He chucked her under the chin. "Maybe next week."

She nodded. "It's not a bad thing to want to do this, right? To want to take care of a baby who doesn't have anyone else in the world?"

"Of course, it's not a bad thing." Mom stopped flipping through the mail. "But that doesn't make it an easy thing either."

"I know it won't be easy." Michelle flattened her good hand against the countertop. "But I am serious about it. I really feel like God is leading me to do this. That He put me here to take care of Grace."

Her parents exchanged a look.

"Okay. Maybe start by showing us how it'll work. We know you've said it several times now. But let's see how it works as we go through all of this, assuming it's even an option when the state finally finds out everything they can about Leah and John and their executor."

"What do you mean, 'show you'?" Michelle frowned.

"We're officially the foster parents." Mom pointed between herself and Dad. "But we're expecting you to step up and act like the parent. You say you want to do this, so we'll let you. We'll work our hardest to try and help you through all the legal stuff, but since this is your idea, it's your responsibility."

Michelle looked down at the sleeping infant in the bassinet next to her. "How hard could it be?"

CHAPTER 3

*I*t took Greg and Michelle almost half an hour to get the base of Grace's car seat moved from Michelle's parents' vehicle to his SUV. Somehow, he had a feeling they were over-complicating it. Once they were all strapped in, Greg aimed the Jeep toward Little Rock. Michelle leaned her head back against the leather headrest. Greg had driven a Jeep since he got his license, but this one didn't rattle and shake like the one he'd driven in high school.

"Tired?" He gave her knee a squeeze, a jolt of awareness traveling through his fingers.

She blinked at him a moment before answering. Had she felt something, too?

"We got four hours of sleep last night." Michelle glanced in the back seat where Grace, at least, was getting more rest.

"That's more than I got. I snuck in a two-hour nap before showering and coming to get you."

"How do you look so alert after only two hours of sleep?"

Greg held up a travel mug and took a sip. The aroma of very strong coffee wafted through the car.

"That smells so good."

He grinned and pointed at the second cup-holder. It held a

similar mug. She quickly snatched it up and took a long drink of the bitter but caffeinated beverage. He chuckled.

"After all these years, I still know exactly what you want first thing in the morning."

"Can I help it my parents started me out early on coffee? It's just like mother's milk to me now." She took another swallow. "Besides, Mom's coffee maker hadn't finished before I had to meet you."

"I remember the first time I saw you drinking it in high school. I thought you'd lost your mind."

"I had to have something to keep me awake through first-period chemistry." She wrinkled her nose. "That subject was seriously boring."

"And you pulled an *A* anyway."

"Of course."

She reached for the cup again with her left hand and cringed as her cast bumped into the metal. With a huff, she blew her brown bangs up off her forehead, a motion he'd seen her do hundreds of times over the years when frustrated with her own forgetfulness. Switching to her right hand, she took another long swallow.

"How long do you have to wear a cast this time?"

"Maybe six weeks. Five, if it heals faster." She wiggled her finger at him. "And just for the record, this time wasn't because of something stupid I was doing. This was due to the airbag shoving my hand back at an unnatural angle."

He nodded. "Because you were probably holding the steering wheel wrong."

"Just because I hold a steering wheel differently than you do doesn't mean I hold it wrong. Just like holding a pencil. There's more than one right way to do it."

"Remember that time you jumped out of the swing at its highest point?"

"You thought I was dead." Michelle smiled.

"You were just lying there, and your face was white. I thought I'd have to break your Mama's heart."

"You almost did, anyway. You burst into the house, screaming that I wasn't moving. She rushed out of there with soap still on her hands from washing the dishes."

"She almost ran me over on her way to you." He laughed.

"That cast was yellow." She traced the edge of the pink one now on her arm.

"Everyone in class got to sign it, but you saved me the biggest spot."

She nodded. "It made everyone think you were my boyfriend."

Would he get to sign this one? She probably wouldn't want signatures all over her arm now—too unprofessional. Too bad. He rather liked the idea of having his name on her arm for all to see. Like staking a claim. What would she think about that?

"How old were we? Seven?"

Her question pulled him back from those dangerous thoughts.

"Beginning of second grade."

Michelle glanced toward the back seat again. Her parents had found a mirror to hang back there so they could see Grace's face.

After a quick scan of his rearview, he motioned toward the dozing child. "Maybe you should join her."

"Nah. I'm good for now."

They were quiet for several miles. It wasn't that far to the city from Cedar Springs. The service was at one that afternoon, but the caseworker wanted to meet with Michelle while she was in the area, so they headed down early.

"Have you talked to Mrs. Winters yet?" Greg asked.

"I'm supposed to meet with her first thing Monday morning." Michelle picked at a spot on her black skirt. Emma Winters was the editor-in-chief of the *Cedar Springs Sun*, where Michelle would soon work. "I touched base with her when I got back to town, to let her know about the wreck and my wrist. She agreed to meet with me at the originally planned time."

"How on earth did you even hear about the job opening up?" Not that he was complaining about her being back. Just curious.

"You know, I interviewed there several years ago, right out of college. It was between me and Hugh Winters, Emma's nephew. She hired him but wanted to hire me as well. She'd been waiting for Richard to retire so she could offer me the position. She got my information from my parents and called me. I accepted immediately."

"Will you make the same as you did? I thought you were pretty settled in Little Rock."

She shook her head. "I've always wanted to move back. I think it's more fun to write when the people reading your column know you. It's more personal."

"You'll be a huge asset to that paper. They definitely need some new blood in there."

"Let's not shed too much of my blood just yet." Michelle nudged him with her elbow. "Hey, how's your sister?"

"Darcy's good. Phillip, too. Can you believe they've been married for six years now?"

"Really? Is she that much older than we are?"

"About four years." Greg frowned at her.

Their families practically raised them all together.

"That's right. She graduated the year before we started high school."

"Yep."

"No kids yet?"

Greg let out a breath. "They want kids, but it's not working. They've gone through some treatments, but no luck yet."

"I'm sorry." Michelle tucked her feet under her. "I can't even imagine how hard that would be."

"It's rough on the whole family."

Grace fussed in the back seat, and Michelle reached around to tuck the pacifier back where it belonged, contorting her body, considering the more convenient hand was in a cast. The seatbelt had to be cutting into her neck. Greg glanced at the rearview.

The baby didn't want to take it at first but seemed to decide it was better than nothing. Grace's eyelids drooped again as she worked the pacifier in her little bow-shaped mouth. Michelle ran a hand over the soft hair on top of Grace's head before turning back to the front.

She met Greg's eyes then looked away. Was she feeling guilty at all about what he'd just told her versus the situation she was in? Why should she be blessed with a sweet little girl like Grace when Darcy and Phillip wanted kids so desperately and couldn't have them? But for some reason, she was convinced God had something in mind when he brought Grace into her life.

DIANE MET them at a small café not far from where the service for Leah and John would take place. Michelle quickly introduced her to Greg and then let her hold Grace for a bit. She was rather proud that the little girl was so healthy and perfect-looking. It was almost like saying to the caseworker, *See? I can do this!*

The woman spread out several papers. "Let me give you a quick update, and I won't take up any more of your time. We've located the friend who Leah and John named as the executor of their wills. His name is Kevin Long. He's unmarried and quite happy staying that way, and he has no interest in taking in Grace. He says a bachelor pad is no place to raise a baby."

Michelle let out a small breath she'd been holding. One step in the right direction.

"Kevin grew up with John. You'll probably see him here today. I think several people are coming from their hometown, Greenbrier. They went to church up there for several years, but it was an older congregation, mostly people who would be grandparent figures and not ready to start over with a new child.

He said they hadn't made many new friends here in the last few weeks. And he doesn't know of any living family for either of them."

Michelle nodded. This all sounded more than promising.

"However, we were able to look at the wills more closely." Diane ran her hand over one of the sheets of paper.

Had they just changed direction? Michelle's heart skipped a beat, and she gripped the edge of her seat under the table.

"They have several stipulations in here as to what they want in the people who adopt their child. First and foremost, their friend Kevin has to approve. Evidently, he was like a brother to John, and John trusted him to make a good decision for their daughter should this situation ever occur."

Michelle made a mental note to be friendly to Kevin.

"Secondly, they want a married couple to adopt Grace. They want her to have both a mom and a dad and the kind of stability that comes from having married parents."

Was that the sound of her world crashing down around her ears? Michelle's heart might as well have stopped altogether.

"Thirdly, but most importantly, they want the adoptive parents to be Christians."

Michelle's heart was definitely still beating, but she was numb all over. She could meet two of the requirements. Could there be any way to get around the third? Surely, something like that wouldn't stand up in a court of law. There had to be a way to keep Grace with her.

"Until Kevin can approve of anyone, he is very happy with the situation we found for Grace. Your family is more than welcome to continue fostering her until something permanent can be arranged." Diane gathered her papers. "I just wanted to fill you in on what we found out, so you can make plans for the future. I know you'll be happy to see Grace placed in a loving family like Leah and John wanted for her."

Greg nudged Michelle. Diane stood, waiting for an acknowledgment. Michelle slowly rose to her feet and clasped

Diane's hand. Then, Diane was gone, and Michelle slumped back in the chair.

"What's wrong?" Greg asked.

"Didn't you hear her? I can't keep Grace."

"Mick."

"She laid it all out. According to their will, the guardian must be married." She waved her hand in the air as if she could summon a miracle. "I'm not ready for that. Even if I had someone in mind."

"Okay." Greg reached over and stilled her hand. "But you still have her for now. And you have no idea what could happen between now and when they get this all figured out. You might even change your mind."

She glared at him, and he held his palms up as if in surrender.

"I know. I know you don't think you will." He leaned forward. "But I also know you want what's best for Grace. Put yourself in Leah and John's shoes. If it were you, wouldn't you want the absolute best for your child, should you no longer be around? What Diane said is true. Married parents tend to have more stability."

"But it's not fair!" She knew she sounded petulant, but she couldn't help it. Every time it looked as though this was what God wanted in her life, another door shut in her face.

"Michelle, pray about it. Give it to God." Greg lowered his head a moment and then looked up again. "If it really is what He wants in your life, He'll work it out."

She took a breath, letting the fresh air sweep some of the anxiety away as she exhaled. "You're right."

"Set this aside for now." He stood and picked up the baby carrier. "You can think more about it after we get through the funeral."

CHAPTER 4

"I know you're not going to remember any of this." Michelle kept her voice to a whisper as they entered the church building where the memorial service was being held for Leah and John. She glanced down at Grace with a sad smile. "But I think you'll be happy to know you were here when you're older."

The little girl blinked big, blue eyes at Michelle as if she understood every word. Greg squeezed Michelle's shoulder, and they made their way to the middle of the room. Michelle had debated sitting in the front since Grace was their daughter, but she wasn't sure how people would take her being there with the deceased's child.

While they waited for the service to start, she studied the pictures in the front of the room. She tried to see where Grace got her nose and the shape of her long fingers. Maybe there was a smidge of Leah's chin in the baby. Or a similarity of John's wavy curls and color in the fine hair on Grace's head.

Michelle absent-mindedly rocked the baby as familiar hymns played throughout the room. It wasn't a large crowd. Several people who looked about the same age as Leah and John gathered toward the front of the room. She assumed they were friends from their hometown, one of them probably Kevin. Would one of them eventually end up being Grace's mom? Michelle quickly looked away again and met Greg's eyes.

"I'm worried about you." A frown wrinkled his forehead as he studied her.

"I'm fine." She shifted Grace to a position easier on her wrist.

He draped his arm around her shoulders, and she leaned back into its comfort. Things quieted down as an older gentleman took his place behind the pulpit and paused for a moment.

"Leah and John weren't very old by this earth's standards." The man shuffled some papers around. "Twenty-four and twenty-five, they lived not even a quarter of the life of Abraham. But they were faithful like he was. Over the years, they leaned on each other as their parents passed due to different diseases. More importantly, they leaned on God. They struggled through years in college, and, starting out as a married couple, surpassed all my expectations."

Several of the girls in the front sniffled.

"Now, today, we're here to celebrate the lives they lived, short though we may consider them. To us, they were friends, fellow Christian brother and sister, co-workers, neighbors. And they were parents-to-be. Their daughter is here today, and I hope she realizes as she grows that her parents already loved her as much as they loved each other and the Lord."

Michelle tried not to notice the various looks sent her way as she sat there with the daughter the preacher mentioned. He went on to talk about how Leah and John had been high school sweethearts and had somehow managed to work and go to school while keeping their love for each other strong enough to make it through the trials the world threw at them. If Michelle had met Leah and John before the wreck, would she have become friends with them?

A slideshow played, showing pictures of the couple as they grew up, married, and as Leah grew with child. They sang several songs about Heaven, and the preacher read a few verses about how when Christians passed away, it wasn't the end. As he finished, he asked if anyone in the audience would like to say a few words about Leah and John.

A man with shaggy hair and a beard rose slowly. He was young, but his face looked old as he stood behind the pulpit and took a breath. He ran a shaky hand over his dark blue blazer as if to smooth down a wrinkle or calm a bunch of butterflies in his stomach.

"John was the closest thing to a brother I had." His voice wobbled a bit, and he took a deep breath before continuing. "When my childhood got bad, his family let me spend as many nights as I needed to. We played on the same basketball team in high school and were roommates our freshman year of college. We pulled pranks, pulled all-nighters, and even pulled his truck out of a ditch a time or two. I thought we'd have years and years left."

He paused for a minute, ran his fingers over his eyes. "I'm going to miss you, John. Leah, too. I always picked at him for marrying his high school sweetheart, but she was the best decision he ever made. I hope one day I can find a Leah for myself."

The man made his way back to his seat. No one else got up. The funeral directors instructed the people to get up row by row and make their way to the front, past the closed caskets and the many photographs scattered around them. Michelle stood on shaky legs when it was her turn. Greg stayed right beside her, his hand on her lower back.

They paused at each coffin, and Michelle whispered, "I'm sorry."

As people milled about after the service, several came to see baby Grace. Michelle reluctantly handed the baby around to the friends of her parents. How much longer would she get to keep this precious child before she had to give up the dream of having her as a daughter? Michelle quickly scanned the hand of every girl who asked to hold Grace—looking for a wedding ring—just to see if she was competition. She tried not to, but her heart looked anyway.

The man who'd spoken about John introduced himself as Kevin. "It's nice to meet the people who are taking care of my charge."

"My parents are officially the ones the state has fostering Grace, but I'm helping." Michelle pointed to the man beside her. "This is my friend Greg."

"Oh." Kevin frowned. "I guess I just assumed y'all were a couple."

"No. Best friends." Michelle waved her hand in a cutting motion. "He was nice enough to offer to drive me today. You know, your town isn't too far from where we live. You'd be more than welcome to come see Grace."

"I'll keep that in mind. Maybe if I had my own Leah, I'd take her in as my own, but I don't think it would be fair to the little girl to force her to live with my bachelor ways. Even I'm not sure my place is sanitary sometimes."

"Bachelorhood has its perks but also has its downfalls." Greg chuckled, although it didn't ring quite as true as normal. Maybe he was simply moved by the service, too.

They traded phone numbers so Kevin could keep in touch as things progressed down the road of finding Grace a new set of parents.

"Take your time." Michelle took the baby as Kevin offered her back. "We're doing just fine as we are. And you want to find the very best home for Grace." She swallowed the lump of disappointment that the home more than likely wouldn't be hers.

Kevin nodded. "Or at least the second-best."

THE RIDE HOME that afternoon was too quiet for Greg's comfort. Michelle fed Grace before they started on their trip, so the baby happily snoozed in the back seat. Michelle stared out the window.

"Two pennies for your thoughts." He quoted their favorite version of the old adage. Growing up, they'd combined the original with the one about putting in their two cents' worth.

She smiled at the saying. Then frowned. "Just wondering if I *would* make a similar request were I in the same position as John and Leah. I know it's easy for me to think that my parents or my brother would just take in any kids I might leave behind, but they didn't have that option, and evidently, they were the first of their friends to marry. None of the girls who asked to hold Grace this afternoon had a wedding ring."

Greg glanced over at her. If he hadn't known her his whole life, he might not have been able to follow that mental leap.

"I couldn't help it." She shrugged. "I just happened to notice each and every left hand that took her out of my arms."

"You're crazy."

"You've already said I hadn't changed. Why does that surprise you?"

"I guess maybe it doesn't." They went several miles more before he spoke again. "You tired?"

"That's a funny question coming from the man who had only a couple of hours' sleep last night. Why don't you look exhausted?"

"Working with the youth group keeps me young." He beat out a rhythm on the steering wheel to accent his joke. "And I'm highly caffeinated right now. I figure I'll crash as soon as I get home, sleep a couple of hours, get up and study my sermons one more time, and then crash again."

"Dad would have come with me today, you know. You didn't have to."

"I know. And they probably wouldn't have mistaken him for your boyfriend."

"Ugh. No kidding. How awkward was that?" She tucked one leg under her and leaned back against the seat.

Greg just shrugged. Had it truly been so awkward? So off-putting? Honestly, he'd been pleased that someone had jumped to such a conclusion.

"How's the whole youth minister thing going?"

She moved on to a new topic, one she probably considered safer.

"I love it, of course."

"Of course."

He could hear the smile in her voice despite her not facing him.

"At first, it was a little weird. Some of the older kids in the group still remembered me being in the group myself. But then I started planning activities like we did back in middle school. Do you remember that youth minister we had? He was the one who made me consider this as a career possibility. He made God come alive for me. Anyway, I'm trying to be a lot like him, though maybe without the drama of how dreamy the girls thought he was."

"Oh, please. I'm sure every girl in your youth group is in love with you."

Greg shook his head. "Well, if they are, they're not telling me. Maybe you could find out and write it in a note like we used to in middle school. Use the old code we came up with, where we wrote everything in Pig Latin and backwards."

"Ugh. Maybe you should get married, so they won't be so tempted to fall in love with you." She playfully punched his arm.

"I haven't found a girl I could convince to love me enough to marry me." He kept his voice soft, hoping she wouldn't hear the yearning in it. "Guess you'll just have to be on the lookout until I do."

"I'll do my best, but it may not come in Pig Latin and backwards."

Her response helped him move past the disappointment. "You're no fun."

"How about upside-down?" She crossed her eyes at him and stuck out her tongue.

"Rather fitting. That's pretty much how you keep my world." And he wouldn't have it any other way.

He dropped Michelle and Grace off in time for dinner. The spring afternoon was turning chilly as clouds rolled in overhead. Together, they once again wrestled the car seat out so it could ride in her parents' car the next day. He carried it into the house with her and greeted her parents.

"You know you didn't have to wait for Michelle to come home to have a reason to come over." Lisa wrapped him in a hug. "You're welcome anytime."

"I know, Mama Lisa." He squeezed her mom's shoulders. They had always referred to each other's mothers with the term of endearment, probably because their moms had been best friends since long before they were born.

Greg stayed only a few minutes, his exhaustion becoming more and more demanding the longer he stood there.

Michelle bumped her arm into his as she walked him back to the front door. "Get some sleep tonight."

"You, too." He chucked her under the chin.

"Something tells me you'll get more than I will."

"Ah, but you don't have to work tomorrow. Your new job doesn't start until Monday."

She grinned. "True."

"See you tomorrow, Mickey."

~

MICHELLE STIRRED from a deep sleep and squinted through bleary eyes at the clock. A little after two a.m. Cries echoed through the monitor as the little green lights flashed and flickered. Michelle sat up, put on her glasses, and shuffled from her room down the hallway where decades of pictures graced the wall of foster kids who'd passed through this household. Would

Mom add a photo of Grace? Or would she get a place with more honor because she would be a grandchild?

She scooped the baby up with her good arm, using her casted hand for balance, and propped Grace on her shoulder as she groggily made her way to the kitchen. Juggling a bit, she grabbed a prepped bottle from the counter and added warm water to the formula.

Back in the living room, she plopped down in the rocking chair and situated the squirming baby. Grace greedily sucked as soon as her mouth found the nipple. Michelle pushed the chair into a steady rhythm.

"Okay, baby girl. This time wasn't quite three hours. How about now let's aim for at least four? Sound good? I have a feeling if Uncle Greg sees us sleeping in church tomorrow, he just might call us out from the pulpit."

Even as she said it, referring to Greg as Grace's uncle seemed right. She rocked back and forth to the rhythm of the grandfather clock on the other side of the room. Grace stared at her with her big, blue eyes as Michelle smiled down at her.

"I know they think I'm crazy for wanting this. But they don't understand. What do you think? Would you like to keep me as your mom? Think we can find a way to fight the court system and win?"

As Grace neared the end of the bottle, she blinked, her eyes slowly drifted closed, and her mouth relaxed.

Michelle sighed and stood up. "Guess you don't find that idea nearly as fascinating as I do. But I plan to try my best, anyway."

CHAPTER 5

*G*race started fussing ten minutes into Greg's sermon the next morning. Michelle quickly grabbed the diaper bag and the baby and made her way back to the nursery. Once the infant had been changed and had a bottle, Michelle discovered she could sit in one of the rockers and listen to the last half of the message. She wouldn't admit it to anyone here, but she hadn't made it to every church service in Little Rock.

As she listened to the words coming through the speaker on the wall, her soul was like a dry desert ground enjoying the rain.

"Just because something happens you think is a bad situation, it doesn't mean something good can't come from it." Greg's voice sounded sure and confident. "No, we shouldn't rejoice that the bad thing happened. But we should rejoice that God will use the situation to help us grow into stronger Christians if we let Him."

He was preaching from James. Greg had always been more spiritually grounded than Michelle. She had to admit the only reason she'd wanted to go to church camp each summer was to meet boys and hang out with friends from past years.

Greg had soaked up the devotionals and led singing and prayers before he was even old enough to be a junior counselor. Michelle was proud of him but a little jealous too. His life seemed to be playing out exactly like he'd planned it, while hers seemed to be on a slower track.

"Things won't always turn out the way we think they should in the end." The sound of him stacking his notes up told her he was almost finished. "Although we know that in the very end, when Jesus comes back, that's when everything will turn out right. But only if you're right with God. Do you know if you're living your life in such a way that you'll end up going home with Jesus, or do you have some doubts about it? We'd love to help you in any way we can."

Michelle wanted to run to the front and ask for help. Things had spun out of control lately, and she wasn't sure which way she needed to go anymore. She knew which direction she wanted, but everything was stacked against her. As the congregation sang the final hymn, she quietly hummed along. The door opened, and a mom with a small child came in for a diaper change. Michelle exchanged smiles and turned her attention back to the closing prayer.

Most of the crowd had cleared out of the auditorium before she made her way to where her parents visited with Greg's family. She one-arm hugged Greg's mom, Sheila, and his sister, Darcy. Everyone was talking about lunch plans, and she quickly agreed that the local diner sounded great. There weren't many eating options in the town of Cedar Springs, but what they did have was delicious.

They walked out together to meet Greg at the door. He said he'd join them at the restaurant since he was still talking to a few more people. Michelle gratefully let Dad lift the baby carrier out of her hands. After a while, it got heavy, even though Grace didn't weigh much.

IT TOOK three tables pushed together to fit their entire group. Michelle smiled as everyone decided where to sit. She ended up in the middle with Grace's car seat propped on a chair between her and Mom. Greg sat on her other side, just like he always had at these get-togethers. She couldn't imagine it being any other way. Darcy and Phillip ended up taking the end next to Greg, and the rest of the parents filled in the gaps.

Michelle looked over the familiar menu. It hadn't changed for as long as she could remember. Today, however, she noticed a label had been placed over one of the original items, and someone had written *red beans and rice*. She frowned as she tried to remember which dish had been there before.

"Dirty rice." Greg's whisper tickled her ear.

"What?"

"It used to say *dirty rice*, but someone got offended. So, they changed it to *red beans and rice*, which technically isn't the same thing, but I guess we're too far from Louisiana for anyone to care." He loosened his tie and slipped it off over his head. His jacket had evidently been left in his Jeep.

"That's crazy."

"Yeah. I think the person who was offended doesn't even live here anymore, but it's too much trouble to go back and remove all the stickers."

The waitress took their orders.

"Chicken strip dinner," Michelle and Greg said at the same time. They grinned at each other and added, "With gravy."

"Someday, you'll have to try something different." Darcy waved her menu at them.

"Why?" Greg asked. "We've found something we like."

"Have you ever had anything different here?" Sheila asked.

"I had a burger once." Michelle twisted her good wrist back and forth. "It was okay. I just like the chicken fingers better."

Darcy shook her head and ordered a chef salad. It was her normal order, too, but Michelle didn't point it out. She knew Greg's sister was good at teasing but didn't always take it in return very well. Greg seemed to know exactly what Michelle was thinking because he nudged her under the table with his foot.

Their families blended almost seamlessly. Her mom, Lisa, and Sheila had been friends since high school. When they married, their husbands, Bryce and Peter, had joined into the friendship, and when the kids came along, they were practically raised as siblings. Michelle had spent more time with the Marshalls than with her extended family. Darcy was like a big sister to her, and she was pretty sure Greg considered her brother, Matt, the same way.

The waitress came back with a tray loaded with their food. As she put down the plates, she stopped at Grace's chair and oohed and ahhed over the baby. Michelle and Mom smiled at the server but tried not to make too big a deal over it with Darcy sitting right there. After the waitress left, everyone settled into their dinners.

Greg reached over and snuck one of Michelle's fries. She swatted his hand, and he made a face at her but ate it anyway.

"You two never change, do you?" Sheila asked.

"I changed clothes yesterday." Greg winked at his mom. "Does that count?"

"No." Darcy pointed at him with a forked tomato. "You still need to do it more than once a week."

"Touché, big sister."

Grace started to fuss, and Michelle leaned over to take her out of the car seat.

"I can take her, Michelle. You still have half your food left." Darcy held out her hands. Michelle reluctantly passed the baby across the table. She hadn't been sure how she was going to hold Grace, feed her, and eat at the same time with only one good hand. But she hadn't wanted to suggest this scenario either, not sure how sensitive Darcy was.

Darcy settled back with the infant, holding her perfectly as Phillip ran his hand over Grace's downy-soft hair. They looked like the perfect family. Michelle looked away as her heart clenched.

Greg squeezed Michelle's knee under the table. Squaring her shoulders, she dove back into her lunch as if nothing were wrong. The odds of her being a mom for Grace were stacked against her, and she needed to face that. She'd have to come up with a plan soon if she wanted to change those odds. But for now, she should relax and enjoy this family time.

"How's your brother?" Greg asked as the rest of their family chatted around them.

"As far as I know, he's off in some foreign country right now, doing his thing. I don't really understand what he does. Just that he goes around showing other people how to use the products his company comes up with. It's all very technical and over my head."

"And you're just a bit jealous of all the world he's getting to see while you're stuck here in small-town Arkansas."

"I told you before. I wanted to move back to Cedar Springs."

"Yes." Greg snitched another fry. "But you also wanted to go put your foot on every continent too. Isn't that what you told me right before we went to college?"

"It would be neat." She lifted a shoulder. She'd honestly forgotten that crazy plan from high school. "Although I'm not too sure about Antarctica."

"But that would be the coolest one." Greg wiggled his eyebrows.

"How 'punny.'"

"Maybe you'll marry someone who will take you somewhere exotic for your honeymoon." Phillip inserted himself into their conversation.

"If I ever decide to get married." Michelle scrunched her face up, then lowered her voice so that only Greg could hear. "I guess I need to if I intend to adopt Grace."

"Would it be so bad if you didn't get to adopt her?" Greg kept his words soft too. Or was that something else keeping his voice so low?

"What are you two whispering about?" Mom leaned over so she could see both of them.

Michelle straightened from where she'd leaned toward Greg to hear him, suddenly aware of how close were. Setting her napkin on the table, she shrugged.

"High school dreams, of course." Greg sopped up the last bit of his gravy with a bite of Texas toast. "And how Michelle is jealous of Matt getting to travel the world."

"I am not." Michelle threw a fry at him.

"Well, I am." Her mom set her glass of tea back on the table. "I keep telling him he needs to take me with him one of these days when he goes to Europe. I just can't talk Bryce into thinking it's a good idea to go there. Imagine all the great shopping we could do."

Michelle was grateful for the change in subject, still smarting from Greg's question. Even if he didn't understand why she wanted this so badly, how could he question her biggest wish right now? He was supposed to be her best friend.

"What's going on?" Darcy snagged Greg's arm outside the restaurant before he could escape to the sanctuary of his Jeep.

The non-stop action of his weekend had finally caught up, and the siren song of a nap was loudly calling his name. But the look on his big sister's face brooked no argument. He tossed his tie across the seat already draped with his jacket and stifled a sigh.

"What do you mean?"

"You and Michelle looked rather cozy." Darcy crossed her arms over her chest. "Yet also, at odds. You've never been at odds. Not since the first time you met her when you were three months old."

"Maybe you're just seeing my utter and complete exhaustion coming out." Greg threw her a half-grin, hoping it would be convincing enough. "I haven't stopped in about three days."

Darcy leaned against the side of his vehicle, just close enough to the open door that he couldn't risk shutting it. "Don't play dumb with me. I know you better than just about anyone else in this world, and I've known for a long time that you felt more for her than she did for you."

His breath rushed out in a whoosh. So much for having hidden that truth from the world. If his sister knew, who else did? Did Michelle?

No.

If she had even suspected such a thing, there was no way she could've maintained their normal relationship all these years. The secret was still safe from the one who mattered most.

"Well?" Darcy tapped a toe.

"There's nothing to tell. Just because I might have stronger feelings than my best friend doesn't mean anything can come of it. You heard her in there." Greg dashed a hand through his hair. "When she talked of marriage, she used the word *if*."

"But she also wants to adopt Grace, yes?"

"Yes." He leaned the back of his head against his open door.

"Sounds like you don't support that choice."

"I honestly don't know." His breath whistled through his teeth. "It's ridiculously complicated. And I can't see how it will work out well. But it's Mickey. How do I do or say anything that might crush her dreams? It goes against every particle inside me."

Darcy was quiet, her lips pursed in thought.

"Do you think it's a good idea for her to adopt Grace?" Greg straightened. Maybe his sister saw something he didn't.

"I think ..." Darcy paused as if working out the exact wording she wanted to use. "I think there's no one in this world right now who loves that child more than Michelle Wilson."

A weight settled over Greg's chest. So, he was wrong.

"That being said," Darcy continued, "I know it's going to be a long and hard road if she makes it happen."

The pressure eased just a tad.

"What do I do, Darce?" Greg kicked at his tire. "I'm more lost than I've ever been in my life."

"You know she's always wanted to move back, right?"

"Ye-es."

"What were you hoping for when you thought about her moving back? Before all of this happened."

"I guess I had a secret hope." Why was it so hard for him to admit this? "I wondered if maybe we'd finally move past friendship."

"Don't give up." Darcy waved at Phillip over Greg's shoulder, probably to let him know she was almost done. "It might not happen right away, not with these additional complications. But keep doing what you do best. Be her friend, Greg. Be there for her. Pray for her. Support her as much as you can. And love her."

As if he could stop.

"And maybe one day she'll see what's been in front of her this whole time." Darcy kissed his cheek and then joined her husband.

Was she right? He slid onto the warm leather seat and revved the engine. Was there still room for hope, even with the baby in the picture?

CHAPTER 6

*E*mma Winters stood five feet even, but everyone in the newspaper office, all five employees—and a few paperboys—respected her like she was seven feet tall. The little gray-headed lady had run this paper since her father retired almost forty years ago. And his father ran it before that. It was no wonder she'd hired her nephew Hugh two years ago when Michelle first applied for one of the main writing positions. The paper was a family business.

Hugh waved at her as she walked across the busy room toward Emma's office. She half-heartedly returned his greeting. It wasn't that she didn't like Hugh. She just didn't always appreciate his positions on things. He was the one who'd run against her for class president her senior year of high school— and he was the one elected. Okay. So, she wasn't totally over that yet.

"Michelle, dear. Come in, come in." Emma stood from behind her intimidatingly large desk.

Papers were strewn helter-skelter across the top of it— clippings of old newspapers, notes and memos in different handwriting, a few laminated columns from the short time she'd been a staff writer too. Michelle shook her hand and sat in the hard, wooden chair as Emma returned to her cushioned one. This office looked like something straight out of a black-and-white movie.

"I'm so glad you're finally here." Emma moved a stack over and flipped through another. "Hugh has been doing okay as the main writer, but I know he could use some help. And, of course, you'll have your own column every Sunday, just like I promised. 'All about Town,' or whatever you planned to call it. I'm sure it will be lovely."

"I've been following your writing these last few years. It's amazing how easy it is to read various columnists without having to subscribe to other papers, now that we have the internet." On the word *internet*, her voice soured a bit.

Michelle nodded. How could Emma see her computer past all the stacks on her desk and through all the sticky notes stuck around the edge of the screen?

"We'll have several meetings a week to make sure everyone knows what stories are running and who wants to write what. It's all very relaxed. We try to be like a big family here—but without the quarrels." Emma waved her hand as if shooing away a pesky fly. "You'll be expected to be at those meetings, of course. Otherwise, people come and go as they need to. The stories aren't in here, after all. Here is just where we write them down and print them."

Michelle got a mental image of Emma as a younger woman, running around town with a pad and pencil, hastily scribbling stories as she noticed them happening. It fit well with Michelle's earlier thought of the office atmosphere and décor. She quickly hid the smile forming on her face and nodded her agreement.

Emma rose and closed the door, then turned to face Michelle, her hands clasped. "There is one more thing I wanted to talk to you about today, dear."

"Oh?" Michelle wasn't sure what to expect from this sudden statement.

"As you know, we have a 'Dear Emma' column. My father

thought it would be cute to name it after his daughter, not even thinking I might grow up to work at the paper one day. I've never actually been the one who answered the letters, of course, but the girl who's been writing it is on maternity leave right now. She'll be unable to focus on writing for a couple of months. I was hoping to talk you into covering it for her while she's out."

"Um ..." How ironic. Emma wanted her to replace someone who just had a baby—while she was basically in the same situation.

"It's nothing—just a hundred words or so, once a week, to answer two short letters. I think our current *Emma* even looks up answers sometimes online to see what other people would say. Then, she chooses which one she likes best and puts it in her own words. Maybe not the best way to do it, but really, this is a simple town. There aren't many problems you'd hear about that you wouldn't already know how to answer. You've got such a good head on your shoulders."

"That's not the kind of writing I do." Michelle nibbled on her bottom lip.

"Let's just try it for a few weeks, and if it doesn't work, I'll find someone else to fill in. But I thought with your hand like it is, it might be something easy you could do until you can pull a full load again."

"I still plan to pull a full load." Michelle resisted the desire to hide her cast behind her back. "This hand isn't slowing me down much at all. I can even still use my camera, as long as I'm careful about how I hold it. But if you can't find anyone else to cover the column, I'm willing to try for at least a few weeks. You may not like my advice, though."

"Oh, honey. It can't be any worse than it was when a pregnant woman wrote it. She was so hormonal. I had to edit her answers every time. The hardest part of the job is that you're not allowed to tell anyone you're the one writing it. It has to be a complete secret."

"I can't even tell one person?"

"Just me." Emma stood up. "Let me show you around the office and get you settled in. I'm sure you're eager to grab some of the assignments from Hugh."

"Sounds great." Michelle followed the editor-in-chief around the small office. It was one big room sectioned off with free-standing half-walls. From any point in the area, a person could catch snippets of at least two phone conversations. Hugh's desk was in the cubical closest to Emma's office. Emma led Michelle to the next one.

"This is your new home. Decorate as you want. The walls are padded fabric, so you can use them as a bulletin board to hold your notes."

The space was fairly simple. An old, scarred desk took up most of it, with a second-hand computer chair. A desktop computer that had to be at least seven years old hummed, and a phone lit up with every ring. She did have access to half of the window in the wall, though, so she could get some natural light. Emma waited with an expectant look on her face.

"Looks perfect."

Emma introduced the other two people in the room—the editor, Charles, and Samantha, who specialized in research as well as writing the obituaries and want ads. Another writer was out covering a high school baseball tournament.

A kitchenette took up one wall, closest to the bathrooms. A coffee pot sat on the counter, but from the strong bitter smell, the liquid was not brewed recently. The cup she'd had at home would have to hold her over until she could get some fresh.

"Hugh, you remember Michelle, of course." Emma led her back to him. "She's ready to get started right away, so you two go through the stories we need covered and see which ones she can do." She lowered her voice. "This afternoon, I'll show you where everything is for that other column."

Emma went back to her office as her nephew raised an eyebrow, but Michelle just shrugged.

"So, here's the caseload for the next couple of days. The

mayor is giving a speech on the upcoming election this fall. The library is having a fundraiser this weekend. The girl scouts are trying to earn more patches with a service project. And the high school is putting on the Spring Play. Mostly just human-interest stuff, but I know that's your specialty."

Michelle nodded. "Any of them you don't want to do? Until I can get my feet under me, I'd like to start this week a little slower, get into the rhythm of the paper here. Every office has a different one."

"Couldn't make it in Little Rock?" He folded his hands behind his head.

"What?"

"There's got to be a reason why you came back. I know it's not the money. This small-town paper is like all the others in the country, dying. The internet is killing print. So, there must be another reason you came back, and I figured you couldn't hack it out there in the city." Hugh grinned at her and leaned back in his chair, which was nicer than the one in her cubical.

"Actually, they tried to talk me into staying." She didn't try to hide the smug look on her face—she could give as good as she got. "I've always wanted to come back home, so when this position opened up, I took it. And I'll take the girl scouts and the play."

Hugh sat up and shoved the memos with the information for the two stories at her. Michelle took three steps to the left and sat in her chair. Not as comfortable as Hugh's probably was, but not as uncomfortable as the ones in Emma's office. She woke her computer and made the calls to meet with people she needed to interview for her stories. She'd show Hugh Winters. He was now on her mental list of people she'd prove herself to, right below Kevin and Greg.

That afternoon, Emma showed Michelle the special box where all the "Dear Emma" letters went. Michelle spent most of the afternoon skimming through letters, making three piles: Not Ever Going to Get Answered, Maybe Some Other Week, and

Maybe this Week. She then went back through the Maybe this Week pile and picked the two that looked easiest to answer.

Back at her desk, she opened a new window on her computer, but as she rewrote the letters into a word processor document, she decided to take Emma's advice and do some research before trying to answer them. She quickly typed in the main topic and searched the internet. Thousands of websites popped up that supposedly had something to do with the issue.

Dear Emma,

> *My mother thinks she has the right to come into my room and go through my things. She reads my texts and stalks me on Facebook. Shouldn't I have the right to privacy?*

> *Sincerely,*
> *Sweet 16 and All Grown Up*

Dear Sweet 16,

Michelle glared at her left hand, which kept her from her average typing speed, and mulled another moment over what to say.

> *It's a cruel world out there, and your mother is trying to protect you. Instead of getting your feathers ruffled, why don't you suggest a compromise? Keep her informed of everything in your life so she doesn't feel the need to snoop. If she knows you're being completely open and honest with her, she won't have as much to worry about. It's what worked for my mother and me.*

> *Sincerely,*
> *Emma*

It wasn't long, but Michelle figured concise was better in this instance, and a sixteen-year-old probably wouldn't want more advice than that anyway. The second letter was from a man trying to convince his fiancée not to get a cat because of his allergies when, in reality, he just didn't like cats. She told him he needed to be honest. Otherwise, even though it was something as simple as whether or not to have a pet, their marriage would start out on the wrong foot.

She saved her work, emailed it to the real Emma for approval, and turned off her computer. It was almost four in the afternoon, enough for day one. Her interviews were scheduled for the two stories she got from Hugh this morning. She grabbed her purse and headed out the door. Almost everyone else had left. The office in Little Rock definitely stayed busy longer, but this slower pace was much nicer.

The day seemed like a success all around—until she walked in the door of her parents' home to the sound of a crying baby.

CHAPTER 7

"What's wrong?" Michelle found her dad pacing the front hallway with Grace on his shoulder.

"She's running a bit of a fever. Your mom is on the phone with the doctor."

Michelle took the baby from Dad and headed toward the back of the house to find Mom.

"Just over a week old." Lisa held up a finger with the hand not holding a phone to her ear. "Yes. We're just fostering her right now. Yes, okay. Okay. Thanks."

Michelle swayed back and forth with Grace. Her little body felt hot but not burning up. The baby still fussed and now had hiccups added to the mix of sobs and cries.

"Let's get her to the doctor. He wants to see her since she's so young. Just to make sure it's nothing serious."

Michelle followed her mother out of the house. Grace fought a little bit as they buckled her in, but they snapped the belts in place and got on the road. Since it was so late in the day, most of the patients had already been seen, and they waited just half an hour before being admitted back to the examination room.

Dr. Bellamy, who'd been her family's physician for as long as Michelle could remember, hadn't changed, with his white hair waving over the top of his head. His face always made her think a bit of Mr. Potato Head, although she wasn't sure if it was the nose or his shape in general. He shuffled in and gently looked Grace over, murmuring soothing sounds.

"Has she been spitting up a lot?"

Michelle and her mom both answered in the negative.

"When did the fever and fussing start?"

"This afternoon."

He listened to Grace's heartbeat and breathing. "I don't see any reason for the fever. She's too young to be teething yet. Looks like she may have a bit of diaper rash forming, so keep an eye on that." Nodding to himself, he hummed a bit as he continued his examination.

"Colic doesn't usually start until about week two, but she may have a bit of it, in which case, you ladies are in for some rough nights. Some doctors believe digestive issues cause colic, so be watching her. If she starts spitting up a lot after eating, she may have some reflux. We can help with that. If she worsens, or if you notice anything else, just give me a call, and we'll get you taken care of. Otherwise, she looks very healthy."

"We did open a different can of formula today. Do you think that could be it?" Mom cocked her head to one side.

"It's possible. Check the ingredients against the ones on the last can if you still have it. There may be something in the new one hurting that little tummy." He patted Grace's middle before handing her back to Michelle.

Just in case, they grabbed another can of the original brand of formula on the way home. Mom figured it was worth a shot, even if they weren't sure yet what had caused this little fever and unhappy spell.

After several more hours of fussing, interrupted by a quick feeding, Grace finally wore herself out a little after ten. Michelle gave her a warm bath, rubbed some diaper rash ointment on her bottom, and gently swaddled her. The baby eagerly took her bedtime bottle, and her eyes closed peacefully—for the first time all day, according to Dad. Mom came in and kissed both Michelle and Grace on the head.

"Someday, you're going to make a very good mommy." Mom's whisper brushed her cheek.

"But not now?" Michelle kept her voice low so as not to stir Grace, but all the frustration and hurt that had built over the last week overflowed from her question. "Why are you and Dad so against me being Grace's mom?"

Mom turned back to face her, leaned against the doorframe, and sighed. "It's not that we're against it. We just worry about you. Being a parent is hard even when you *do* have a husband. You're suggesting going it alone. That's not easy. Not to mention exactly what Leah and John didn't want for their daughter."

Michelle opened her mouth to protest.

Mom held up her hand. "Your father and I are here to help now. But what if you hadn't moved here and had that wreck anyway? You'd still be working your job at the paper in Little Rock, still living in an apartment. There's no way the state would have let you take this baby home since you've never been through the home studies and training they require for fostering children.

"If and when you accomplished all that, you'd have to put her in a daycare program while you worked. What would've happened today if she'd been in daycare instead of with us? Would you have been able to get away from work to take her to the doctor?"

"I work a fairly flexible job, Mom. I could have gotten away." Michelle rolled her eyes.

"What if you were right in the middle of an interview with someone important? You could just leave right then and there?"

"Mom, this is Cedar Springs. Everyone would understand."

"And your high school nemesis Hugh Winters would be the one who picked up where you left off and finished the story you'd been working on. He'd get all the credit, and you'd add one more reason to your list of why you don't like him." Mom raised an eyebrow.

"I don't have a list anymore." Michelle almost rose from the chair out of frustration, but Grace stirred, and she stopped herself. "You threw it away after high school."

Her mom continued to give her *the look*, the one that always got to the truth of the matter.

"Okay, maybe there's a mental list, but it's a short one."

"The fact that you have it at all proves to me you're not ready for something as serious as parenting. You've still got some growing up to do, and that's okay. Right now, you need to learn how to accept that you can't have what you want in this situation and start letting go of that little girl, so your heart doesn't break too badly when someone else adopts her." Mom gave her another kiss and turned toward her room.

Michelle sat in the rocking chair with Grace for a long time after her mom left. The baby was finally sleeping, and Michelle knew she needed to be in bed too, while she could. Grace would want to eat again in a few hours. She just couldn't get the conversation out of her head. Did her parents really think she wasn't grown up? Did they think she was just playing at being a mom right now but not taking it seriously?

"How are we going to prove to them we can make this work?" she asked the baby.

Grace continued to slumber.

WALKING BACK through the doors of Cedar Springs High School was like a trip down memory lane. The smell hadn't improved over the last few years. Michelle wrinkled her nose as she passed the bathrooms in the front of the building.

Taking her time, she meandered past old photos of high school dream teams and senior class portrait compilations. She found her class and quickly searched out her picture. Her senior photos could have turned out better, but it looked enough like her that she couldn't deny it.

Greg's was much better. Boys had it easy when it came to photos. They didn't have to worry about hair or makeup or what their lips looked like if they pursed them a certain way. Most of them didn't even smile.

She braced herself before entering the office—despite knowing she wasn't in trouble this time—and signed the guest register.

The secretary, Mrs. Fitts, had been old when Michelle was in high school, but she looked exactly the same. "Here's your name tag, dear. It's been a while since I've seen you, but I still remember."

Michelle hadn't been in the office *that* often. She offered a grin as authentic as she could muster.

"The auditorium is the same place. Not sure we could move it if we tried." Mrs. Fitts cackled a bit at her own joke. "Just down the hallway here and then take a left. The double doors will be on your right. Let's see." She craned her neck around to look at the ancient clock on the wall. "Yes. They should be in there now. Second period."

Snippets of history and algebra classes tickled Michelle's ears as she walked down the mostly quiet halls. Several students, hall passes in hand, gave her strange looks as she passed them.

At the end of the corridor, she took a left and then pushed through the auditorium doors. The familiar scents took her back to tenth-grade drama class, a little musty with a hint of old popcorn and lots of stage makeup. The plays here weren't Broadway-worthy, but the drama teacher had them polished to the point it was worth the five-dollar Saturday matinee admission price.

This year, they were performing *To Kill a Mockingbird*. Michelle slid into a seat halfway back and watched for a few minutes. She caught pictures as the kids acted out their lines and ironed out the wrinkles before the show's performance this weekend.

Ms. Steele, the drama teacher, spotted Michelle during a break and waved her on up.

"Mind if I get a few photos?"

"No stage fright here." The teacher motioned to several actors hamming it up. "Shoot away."

Michelle took a shot of the whole cast standing in front of the backdrop. As students backstage prepped costumes or worked on props, she snapped more photos. She even caught one of a boy working the lights as he practiced turning the spotlight on and off.

After getting several quotes from the main characters and the teacher, she had enough to write the article. She thanked them for their time and zipped her camera back into her bag. Even though it was a little awkward with her hand in a cast, she'd managed to capture some nice images. Maybe they'd be enough to impress her boss.

She pushed through the auditorium doors and collided with a solid chest. The arms belonging to the muscled torso straightened her as she wobbled between it and the door. She caught her balance and looked into the eyes of her best friend.

~

"WHAT ARE YOU DOING HERE?" Greg asked at the same time as the woman in his arms.

In his arms.

Loathe as he was to let go, he stepped back and helped Michelle straighten the strap over her shoulder.

"Article on the play." She motioned behind her.

"Nice. It's my monthly day to eat with my high school youth group members. Next week is middle school." An idea popped in his head that would keep her here longer. "Want to join us?"

"Um."

"You know you miss the cafeteria food." He playfully nudged her shoulder.

"Oh, yeah. There's a selling point for you."

"Come on. You have to eat lunch somewhere. Do you have time?" Please let her have time.

"Sure." She smiled. "I don't have to back at the office until later this afternoon."

The bell reverberated through the halls as they walked toward the back of the building. Students filled the area instantaneously, their voices echoing off the linoleum, lockers slamming, laughter and footfalls everywhere. Michelle squeezed a little closer to Greg.

"What are you scared of?" He draped his arm across her shoulders. "You used to own these halls."

"I'm not afraid of anything except getting smushed. I don't seem to remember high school the same way you do, but I do remember we didn't really pay attention to anything outside our own little world."

"Come on. I usually meet the kids just inside the cafeteria."

The scent of old fry oil, milk, and bleach hung in the air. Their shoes stuck a bit to the floor as she stepped out of the way. Teenagers poured into the large room in groups and clusters and, occasionally, one by one. The area and setup were the same as when they'd attended. Different cliques filed into their usual spots. Greg pulled her over to his youth group.

"These kids were in elementary school just the other day, right?" Michelle stage-whispered. "Have I been gone that long?"

"Just long enough for them to grow up." He motioned to the line to order. "Come on. Menu today is cardboard pizza, soggy French fries, and chocolate pudding that usually needs a bit more sugar."

"There's a five-star menu for you," Michelle muttered.

But, she grabbed a tray and seemed to eat with relish. Did she remember all the fun times they'd had in here, too?

"You're coming to the baseball game tomorrow, right GM?"

Trevor, a lanky teenage boy with more spots on his face than a pepperoni pizza, leaned forward, almost knocking over someone else's drink.

"I promised, didn't I?"

"What about the play?" Star, an aptly named junior, grinned shyly at Michelle. "Plays are great for a date night."

Michelle's eyes widened.

"Which part are you playing again?" Greg quickly steered the conversation in another way. Much as he'd love to have a date night, it didn't look to be an option any time soon.

"We're still doing the end-of-school thing, right GM?" Mack leaned his chair back on two legs. "You promised that scavenger hunt this time."

He volleyed the conversation, answering questions, listening as they talked about the events in their lives. Michelle sat quietly beside him, but she didn't appear terrified anymore. Just taking it all in.

When the bell rang, the kids quickly packed up, quite a few hugged Greg, and headed back out into the hallway.

"Why couldn't you have been my youth minister?"

Michelle followed him to the window, and they put their trays on the conveyor belt that took them back to the kitchen.

"Because I was in the youth group the same time you were?"

"I guess that makes sense."

"GM, huh?" Michelle bumped his arm as they meandered back down the now quiet hallways. "Should I start calling you that?"

"What do you think?"

"I think I still like Greg-o."

"Don't even think—"

She smirked. "I'm saving it for when I really need to get back at you for something."

They checked out through the office and stepped back into the real world. Michelle loaded her things into the rental car and turned, leaning against the door. In the natural light, her bruises had mostly faded, but now dark circles framed her beautiful blue eyes. Where had the vivacious young woman he knew so well gone?

"What?" She brushed at her face. "Is there pizza sauce or something?"

"The sunshine is bringing out things the fluorescents didn't. You look worn out. You okay?" He hesitated, then reached out and traced the purplish bags.

"Rough night." She looked down. "Didn't sleep much between Grace and something my mom said right before bed."

"Need to talk it out?"

Michelle closed her eyes and turned her face up to the sun. "I'd love to, but I probably should get back, get this article typed up, and edit the pictures."

"What about tonight? Need a pizza night?"

"That sounds lovely, but I have no idea if Grace would let it happen. She fussed pretty much all day yesterday and several hours throughout the night too. There's no way I could take her to Luigi's."

"I could bring it to you. We can picnic on your back porch like we did when we were cramming for midterms."

"That sounds amazing. Would you be willing to do that?"

She had to ask? "Anything for my best friend."

He wrapped her in a hug, wishing he didn't have to let go, and sent her back to work. She drove away, taking a piece of his heart with him, like always. As glad as he'd been to bump into her and gain the promise of seeing her again this evening, it almost made it harder than the times they were apart. If he'd known how hard it would be to see her so often and still not be more than friends, would he have wished so fervently for her to move back?

A thousand times yes.

～

"VERY GOOD. THAT WILL DO NICELY." Emma didn't even look up when Michelle stopped in her office to make sure the editor received her article. The older woman quickly scanned her computer screen just long enough to make sure it was there, not even mentioning the pictures that had turned out so well. She waved her hand in the air. "If you'll excuse me, dear."

Michelle had never seen Emma Winters so distracted, especially from something to do with the paper. She'd always been a bit of a flibbertigibbet but could reign in her flightiness when it came to the job. Michelle kept her shoulders straight and headed out the door.

Hugh nodded as he passed her on his way in. She tried to ignore his aunt's warm greeting as if she hadn't another thing on her mind. Michelle gathered her things and shut down her computer for the day. She had pizza and Greg-time waiting for her. She'd worry about this tomorrow.

Greg would help her figure things out. He always did.

CHAPTER 8

*G*reg kept the back-porch swing moving in a steady rhythm. Michelle leaned against the armrest on her side, her legs up on the bench. Her parents had made the swing extra-large so more people could fit. Tonight, it just held three: him, Michelle, and the baby in her lap. Grace's day had evidently been better, and she dozed sweetly now.

A thunderstorm moved in shortly after Greg arrived with their favorite pizza—ham and pineapple with extra cheese. They sat on the back porch and watched the rain drip from the roof in companionable silence.

It was a far cry from the way they used to sit here, laughing and goofing off instead of studying for midterms. Fortunately for both, they'd been good students and hadn't needed much studying. Otherwise, they might still be stuck in ninth grade.

Her mom came out with freshly baked cookies. She traded Michelle and took Grace with her.

"You don't have to take her, Mom. I was about to bring her in and put her down."

"You just relax. You were up with her most of last night." Her mom continued into the house without waiting for an answer.

"That explains the circles under your eyes." Greg gently

traced one. "Or that could just be a remnant of the bruises from the airbag."

"Ugh. It's been over a week now. How long do bruises last?" Michelle ran her hand across her eyes.

"Considering how hard that airbag probably hit you, count yourself blessed you didn't get a broken nose."

"I do consider myself blessed." Michelle ducked her head.

"Mickey, you know what I mean. I'm sorry."

Greg leaned over until he could see her eyes. Her gaze slowly met his, and a grin spread across her mouth. He'd always had the ability to make her smile, even when she didn't want him to.

"So, is that all that's bothering you? Just lack of sleep? Didn't you say something about your mom?"

"Yeah. She said some pretty harsh things to me last night." Michelle rested her head against the chain.

"You seem to be getting along okay now." Greg motioned with a cookie.

"She made those for you, and you know it." She pointed a finger at him. "Besides, we've seen each other a total of about ten minutes today. It's hard to fight in such a short amount of time."

Greg raised an eyebrow, and she stuck her tongue out at him.

"So, what did she say?"

"She said I need to grow up."

Greg rocked the swing back and forth, back and forth. The words tripped through his head, and he tested several answers, wanting to make sure he got it right. If he'd learned anything from working with teenagers during the last few years, it was the importance of phrasing.

As the rain let up, frogs began their evening song out in the yard. Under the tree next to the fence, an occasional firefly glimmered before hiding again.

"I notice you're not arguing." Michelle nudged him with her foot.

"I guess I need some context. I'm sure she didn't just look at you and say, 'Grow up, Michelle.'"

"No. First, she told me I'd make a good mother someday."

"I definitely agree with that. I see the way you handle Grace. You'll make a great mommy." Greg rested his arm on the back of the bench. That part was easy to admit, even if he wasn't sure the current situation was the best way for her to enter motherhood.

"So, I asked her why she didn't think I could be a great mommy now, why she and Dad don't seem to have any faith in me. And she told me she thought I still needed to do some growing up."

"Because ..." Greg motioned with his hand for her to spill the rest.

"Because she pointed out Leah and John didn't want their daughter adopted by a single person. That they wanted a married couple. And that even if that weren't the case, I would still have issues raising a daughter by myself. She asked what would have happened if I hadn't moved here, if I didn't have my parents to help.

"And then she said I couldn't just leave in the middle of an important interview for an article because it would allow Hugh to take my place." Michelle slumped her head to her knees. "She made me admit to my list."

Greg threw his head back and laughed, setting the swing into an irregular rhythm. "The list. How could I forget that list? Tell me, who else besides Hugh is still on it?"

"I'm not telling you that." Michelle sat up and scowled. "It's not like I have it written down."

"But it's still in your head. You're still keeping tally marks as if life is a competition, and you have to come out on top."

His description stemmed from his memories of high school. The list began when Michelle wanted to be class president, and Hugh had run against her—and won. Back then, the list had been on paper in the back of her math folder. Hugh's name was first, with others added whenever they did something that offended her.

As time went on, she would add tally marks beside a name if that person did something else to make her mad. And stars if she'd gained an achievement they'd both been striving for. That physical list might have been gone for years, but the principal of it remained in the back of her mind, full of tallies and stars, even if the only name still occupying it was Hugh's.

"Just because you might be close to right doesn't mean I have to admit it." She crossed her arms.

And by her saying that, he knew he was.

"Mickey, seriously, Hugh isn't that bad of a guy. He's even come to church a few times since he started dating Vanessa."

"Vanessa Winthrope?"

"Yes."

"The most popular girl in school is dating Hugh Winters?"

"Mickey, we're not in school anymore. No more cliques, no more *most popular* or *most likely to succeed*. We're supposed to be actually succeeding by now." He poked her shoulder, frustrated he had to remind her of things he tried to instill in his youth group.

"I'm still trying to wrap my head around the prom queen dating the boy who's been at the top of my list for as long as I can remember." She shook her head. "I just can't picture it. I guess I'll have to see them together."

"You're sort of rotten, ya know?"

"But you're not supposed to notice because you're my best friend." Michelle tossed a chocolate chip at him.

He grabbed her toes and tickled, remembering the spots that got her giggling.

"I give!" she shrieked.

He let her catch her breath before returning to the serious conversation. "So, back to your mom's admonition from last night." His voice was all seriousness again.

Michelle sighed. "It just feels like I'm the only one who thinks this can work. It's the first time in my life my parents haven't looked at me and said, 'We support you completely. You can do anything you set your mind to.'"

"I know you don't want me to ask you this, but have you prayed about it?"

"Of course, I have. I'm not a complete heathen just because I moved away for a few years."

Greg held up his hands. "I never said that. But are you praying the right thing?"

"What are you talking about? I don't remember reading that there's a right thing to pray for. Just that we should ask for what we desire, and if our faith is strong enough, then God will make it happen."

"It may not say, 'Only pray for this and not that,' but the Bible does point out that God's not going to just give you what you want." Greg shrugged. "Paul asked for his thorn in the flesh to be removed, and God said, 'No.'"

"This isn't a thorn in the flesh. I don't have cancer or something. I'm just trying to do right by this baby." She slammed her hands down on the seat. "How is that wrong?"

Her angst twisted his heart, but he also knew she needed to look at the situation from more than one angle. As her friend, he couldn't simply stand back and support her in something so serious if he didn't at least admonish her to think it through. And it tore him up that for the first time in their lives, he couldn't back her one hundred percent. Of course, he couldn't leave her feeling completely defeated, either.

"Maybe it's not. And maybe God will show you a way to make it happen. But until that comes, you should stay open to other possibilities too."

They sat quietly. She was obviously mulling it over in that hard head of hers. Would she listen to his advice or keep pushing ahead, no matter what?

"Do you think I'm doing the wrong thing in wanting this?" She looked Greg full in the face.

He'd always been truthful with her, even when it hurt. He

didn't want to add to her ache—he wanted to ease it. Why was this so hard?

"Tell me why it's so important to you."

Thoughts flitted across her pretty face, but he couldn't decipher any of the emotions he saw there. If he had to guess, she wasn't telling him everything. When had their relationship added walls? And how did he tear them down again?

"I told you why the other day. It's the right thing to do. I can't explain it more than that."

"Then, I'm not sure, Mickey. I want to think you're making the best decision for not only you, but also for Grace."

Her shoulders slumped, and he almost wished he could take the words back. But life didn't work that way. And the truth hung between them. Darcy was right. He and Michelle had somehow gotten on different wavelengths.

"I'm praying for you." He kissed her forehead and left her on the back porch.

CHAPTER 9

"Kevin called. He wants to see Grace this weekend." Michelle stood at the back of the church building after Wednesday night Bible study.

Greg sat next to her with Grace in his arms, making funny faces at the baby. "That'll be good."

Did Greg think it would be good because Kevin should be in Grace's life? Or because it might move things along faster at getting Grace a new home?

Their disagreement the evening before left a sour taste in her mouth long into the night. They hadn't had a fight ever. Their conversation hadn't really been one, either, but it hurt just as much. Because, for the first time in their lives, they weren't in complete agreement. And that bothered her more than what her mother had said about growing up.

"Yeah." Michelle sighed. "I'm hoping to talk to him and see how strongly he feels about the whole married thing. I mean, Grace's parents said whoever adopted her had to have a spouse, but first and foremost, must be approved by Kevin. What if he approves of someone single more than a couple?"

"What if he won't?" Greg didn't even look her way.

"What is it with you?" She put her hands on her hips. "You

used to go along with all of my plans. Have things changed that much over the last couple of years?"

"Mickey, seriously. This isn't just about you. It's also about Grace. Her parents wanted her to be adopted by people who were married. They didn't see any of this coming, couldn't have known anything about you. But they laid out their wishes just in case. You have to respect that." Greg handed Grace back to Michelle.

She gently laid the baby in the carrier and buckled her in.

"You're right. They didn't know me. So, I guess I just need to get to know Kevin this weekend. It's the next best thing to getting to know Leah and John."

Greg shook his head. "You're so stubborn."

"And?"

"Nothing. Just thought you might need to be reminded."

She smirked at him. "What does that say about you? You're my best friend."

"Who knows?" He looked away for a minute. "What's the word on your car?"

"Totaled. Dad and I haven't had a chance to go shopping for a replacement yet. Not sure what I want."

"A Jeep." He pointed with his thumb out the window at his.

"That's your car."

"And it's a great one. The teenagers think I'm cool when I take the top off."

"Well, that's the best reason in the world to get one." She rolled her eyes. "I, of course, want all the teenagers to think I'm cool."

"What can I say?" Greg shrugged and grinned.

"I'm sure my dad is already shopping around. You know how he is. When he helped me get my first car, I'd keep thinking we'd found *the one*, only to discover he'd found some little thing wrong with it, and off we'd go to another dealership. It took three months before he finally relented and let me buy the vehicle I wanted in the first place."

Greg laughed. "The Toyota. With the back door that wouldn't open. That car saw a lot of miles."

"It was a good car." She smiled at the memories.

"How much longer until the cast comes off?"

"Way too long." Michelle held up her hand. "They said probably six weeks for this thing, and it's only been a little over one. Maybe by my birthday."

"Your birthday is at the end of July, and it's only April now. That's more than six weeks, Drama Queen."

"What? First, I'm stubborn, and now I'm a drama queen?" She propped her hands on her hips.

"I call it like I see it."

She placed the back of her good hand against her forehead and took on a thick Southern-Belle accent. "I just can't imagine whatever you could be speaking of, sir. Little ol' me, dramatic?"

"Mm, hmm." He snickered like she knew he would.

Grace fussed a little, and Michelle looked down. "Guess it's time to go."

"Yeah. Call me if you need to talk this weekend." Greg squeezed her arm. "Or before."

Michelle headed out to meet up with her parents in the parking lot. As she pushed through the doors, though, she bumped into someone. She stepped back and looked up into Hugh Winters's eyes.

"Hey, Michelle." He glanced at the carrier on her arm. "Cute kid. I didn't know you were married."

"I'm not." Michelle shook her head. "She's a foster child." She purposely left out the rest of the story. If she'd wanted him to know more, she'd have told him her first day at work.

"Oh. Well, um, it was nice seeing you."

She nodded and sidestepped him as Vanessa joined him. Even after seeing them together, she still found it hard to believe and shook her head.

～

MOM AND DAD chatted with Kevin on the back porch. He held Grace in his arms and couldn't seem to take his eyes off of her. Michelle watched them through the kitchen window as she mixed up a new pitcher of lemonade. Her phone buzzed, and she pulled it out of her pocket—a text from Greg.

Sending prayers of peace your way

She wasn't sure what to make of him anymore. They had great moments when it seemed there'd never been a time gap in their friendship. Other moments felt like a lifetime had passed since they'd spent any time together. He was the one thing about coming back here that she'd counted on to be the same. She hadn't expected the town to change much, though she'd known it would be different living here as an adult.

But Greg was supposed to be her constant.

She dropped her spoon in the dishwasher and carried the tray with the pitcher and four glasses out the back door. Dad quickly took the tray from her, and Michelle silently sent him a look of thanks. Though her hands were still fairly capable, that tray had been harder to grip than she expected.

"She just looks so much like Leah." Kevin traced Grace's face.

"How long did you know Grace's parents?" Mom shifted in her chair.

"I grew up with John. Leah came along when we were in high school. You never really expect high school sweethearts to last, but they sure did. And life threw some pretty hard curve balls at them. Still, John found his way to God and took the rest of us with him. It's not right that he isn't here to enjoy this."

"Their parents are all deceased too?" Dad set his glass aside.

"Yes. Her mom had breast cancer, and her dad died when she was very young. I think he was in the army. His parents died in a car accident too. Back when we were in college." Kevin accepted the glass held out to him. "They'd been through so much."

Everyone was quiet for a while. Several birds chirped in a tree in the backyard. Michelle scanned the branches to see where the sound came from, but she couldn't figure it out. Sort of like the puzzle her life seemed to be right now—she had the sound but no picture.

"How is the search for parents for Grace going?" Dad cut a look at her and then looked away. Probably guilty for asking such a heartbreaking question.

"The caseworker had me meet several different families during the last week. There's a long waiting list for families who want a newborn. But none of them have felt right. I know you guys probably want your life back. It can't be easy caring for a baby again."

"It's no problem." Michelle waved her hand. "She's a sweetie."

"We just want what's best for her." Mom gave a rather forced-looking smile.

Her parents chatted for a while longer and then went inside. Michelle scooted to the chair closer to where Kevin sat holding Grace. She watched his fingers slowly run over Grace's hair as if mesmerized.

"I got some pretty good photos of her the other day. You should take a few with you when you go this afternoon."

Kevin looked up. "That would be great. Thanks."

How should she broach the subject of her adopting Grace? How should she bring it up? She was supposed to be making friends with Kevin so he would trust her enough to give his stamp of approval. Instead, she sat as if she were mute.

"I guess I'm not good company. Still in shock from losing John and Leah, maybe. Something just told me I needed to come see her this weekend." Kevin glanced up from staring at Grace.

"No worries."

"It's a huge responsibility, going to meet all these people who think they want to adopt Grace. I look at them and keep thinking, *But they're not John and Leah.* How can they be good enough if they're not John and Leah?"

Michelle frowned. "You're not going to find anyone who will match John and Leah exactly."

"I know that in my head." Kevin stared out across the yard. "It's my heart that keeps looking for them in all these people."

Silence reigned again.

"She's so perfect, isn't she?" Kevin motioned to Grace.

"We've come to love her." Michelle reached over and caressed the baby's tiny hand. She watched her father playing with Grace earlier and suddenly knew what he would be like as a grandfather. Grace had wrapped him around her finger. Mom wasn't far behind.

"It can't have been easy for you to take her in after everything. I mean, you didn't come out of that wreck completely unscathed."

"I came out with a few bruises and a broken wrist. And I felt like it was the right thing to do, to take her in. Like there was a connection between us because we were in the same wreck."

"Well, I appreciate it more than you'll ever know. It was enough of a blow to hear that they'd been killed, but to find out I was the one they'd named guardian of their daughter—I just about fell over. I have no idea what possessed John to do such a thing."

"Maybe he knew you'd want the best for his daughter, just like he did." Michelle studied him, once again trying to find the courage to speak her heart.

"Maybe."

Michelle had to know her chances. Her stomach roiled with the words unsaid, until they became volcanic, pushing their way up her throat, wanting to explode.

"Kevin, I want to adopt Grace."

His head jerked up.

"I know I don't meet all the requirements yet, but I do plan to get married in the future. And I love her. Having her here the last, well, almost two weeks now, has been such a great experience for me. I know you can't decide anything right away, but I wanted you to be aware."

Kevin shook his head. "I'm not sure I could go against John

and Leah's wishes about the people adopting Grace being married. I mean, a girl like you, I'm sure you'll find someone great and everything, but how old will Grace be by then? How long will she go without having a daddy?"

Michelle opened her mouth, but Kevin held up his hand.

"I know I don't know you. We've only met a couple of times now, but Michelle, are you sure you want this? I mean, really sure? You didn't even know Leah and John. Why are you so adamant about adopting their daughter?"

"I think God put me there for a reason that night. He saved me from that wreck. I can't think of another reason for that. John and Leah sound like they were much better people than I am. Why should He take them and not me?"

"Only God can answer that." Kevin shook his head. "But I can tell you right now, there may be more than the reason you think He's given you. I'll pray about it, but I want you to be praying about it, too."

"Really?" Michelle gripped the edge of her seat. "You'll put me down as a real consideration?"

"I said I'd pray about it. And I will. But I can't promise anything yet. Like I said, this is the hardest thing I've ever done. I want to make sure I choose what's best for Grace."

Michelle didn't care what happened the rest of the afternoon. Her heart was lifted. Kevin said he would pray about it. Surely, God would put in Kevin's heart what He'd put into hers. Right?

CHAPTER 10

*M*ichelle's hands shook. More as she neared the intersection. She'd driven since the wreck. But not at night. Why was she so nervous?

A green light.

She pressed the accelerator.

A motorcycle.

From nowhere, it cut across the path.

She swerved.

Too late.

The wrong way.

Headlights blinded her.

She sat straight up in bed, her heart racing. Only a dream. She threw her covers off and went to the bathroom to splash water on her face. A glance in the mirror showed her bruises almost gone, but dark circles remained under her eyes. Probably because she hadn't gotten enough sleep in more than two weeks. She patted her skin dry and started back to bed.

Have you prayed about it? Greg's question echoed in her head. She sat down in her chair by the window and curled her feet under her. From this vantage point, the moon cast a glow through her curtains where it hung above their backyard.

She'd grown up in this house. Her bedroom had changed through the years, becoming more mature as she did, but little pieces of her childhood remained. A photo of Greg and her, their arms thrown around each other's shoulders, on her bedside table. They'd probably been in the sixth grade in the picture, but you could tell that their friendship would last a lifetime.

Many an hour had been spent in this chair late at night during high school. She'd stayed up studying or writing in her journal. Every now and then, angst over a boy would keep her awake into the small hours, pouring out her heart in petition and tears to God.

Why wasn't she doing the same thing now? Shouldn't she be praying as hard right now as she had back then for some relationship she'd known deep down inside her wouldn't last longer than a month or two? Or even harder?

She stared back out at the moon and contemplated what to say. Greg suggested she pray not only for what she wanted but also for God's will to happen. And Kevin had said he would pray about the situation but not necessarily that she'd be the answer. What should she pray?

"God, I don't know what to ask for. You know what I want in this situation. Show me what needs to happen."

It didn't seem sufficient, but it was all she could come up with. She'd just have to trust the Holy Spirit to interpret the rest. Her heart calmed down some now, and she could probably get back to sleep, but Grace would more than likely wake her up again in a few minutes. Michelle stood and padded down the hallway to check on the baby.

The moonlight drifted through the window and seemed to make the infant's head glow. Her even breathing held a peace like nothing else Michelle had known. She slowly lowered herself into the rocker and pushed back and forth to the rhythm of the clock in the living room. Growing up, she'd considered the *tick-tock* to be too loud, but now she found its familiarity comforting.

She looked up to see her mom standing in the doorway. "You okay?"

"Had a bad dream. I figured it was about time for her to wake up anyway, so I thought I might as well stay awake."

Her mom nodded. "Want to talk about it?"

Michelle followed her mom to the kitchen, where they wouldn't rouse the baby before she woke on her own. Her mom fixed two small glasses of milk and passed over the container of cookies she'd made the day before. They each perched on a stool, and Michelle smiled at memories of many nights sitting just like this growing up. Her mom had always been there for her.

"What was the dream about?" Her mom took a bite of chocolate chunk.

"The wreck."

Mom nodded.

"I keep seeing it over and over again in my head and wonder what could I have done differently? How could I have saved their lives?"

"Michelle Denise, you have got to quit thinking like that." Her mom squeezed her arm. "There's nothing you can do now to change the fact that Leah and John died. It wasn't your fault, and dwelling on it won't change a thing."

"I can't get it out of my mind." Michelle put her head in her hands as if to rub the image from her eyes. "It just plays out over and over again."

In an instant, she was wrapped in her mother's arms. Michelle leaned into the comfort. It didn't make everything better, but it did help it hurt a little less. They both looked up as Grace cried from the other room. Michelle started to rise, but her mother gently pushed her down.

"I'll get her." Her mom padded quietly through the doorway.

Michelle crumbled a bite of cookie into crumbs. It was a shame because her mother made some of the best treats in the world, but her fingers seemed to need to demolish something.

She brushed the crumbs onto a napkin and threw them away as her mom returned with a fussy baby.

"Go back to bed." Her mom efficiently began to fix a bottle. "I've got this tonight."

"You said it was my job to take care of her."

"And tonight, I'm telling you it's my job to take care of you. Go to bed. I love you."

"I love you, too, Mom." Michelle padded back down the hallway to her room, listening to the sound of her mom singing to Grace. After a few seconds, she picked out the tune and recognized the song, "Jesus Loves Me."

Tears slid down her cheeks as she laid back down in bed. Three weeks ago, she had her life planned out exactly like she wanted it. She'd live with her parents a few months while she got her feet under her at her new job. Then, she'd get her own place, continue to work her dream job, and maybe even find a man she could love for the rest of her life. After a year or two of dating, they'd get married and start their family together. That's how things were supposed to go.

Then, a motorcycle ran a red light.

What was her strategy now? She wasn't sure anymore. Her dream job was great, but it wasn't turning out quite like she'd expected. Hugh was still there, annoying as ever, and Ms. Emma seemed so distracted this last week. It worried Michelle.

Since she now had a baby to think about, she'd have to live with her parents indefinitely, and there was no way she could do it by herself. She admitted it. As for finding a man, she couldn't even think about it. Which was a big part of the problem.

"God, I need a new plan." She aimed her whisper at the sky. "Help me figure out what direction to take. I can't do this anymore. I feel so lost. Help me, please."

~

"WHAT'S ALL THIS?" Michelle asked Samantha.

The girl had spread colored pictures of rabbits all over the conference room table before their morning meeting. Michelle was the second to arrive.

"The yearly Easter contest. We run the picture of the bunny and ask the kids to send in their decorated versions. Then, we all vote on who we think did the best job. We also have to pick a second and third place and a runner-up. So, start looking. This may take all morning. It usually does."

"What does the winner get?" Michelle held up one with more colors on it than she knew existed in the crayon world.

"A gift card to the dollar store. It seems a little silly, but the kids go for it every year, anyway. Maybe the fact that we have more entries this year will cheer Ms. Emma up. She's been worried about our circulation being down."

"Is that what's been bothering her?"

"At least part of it." Samantha looked as if she might say more, but Charles and Hugh walked in just then.

Both men groaned.

Hugh dropped his messenger bag in a chair. "Again? Didn't we just do this?"

"No." Samantha moved two that were mostly done in blue next to each other. "Last time was the Santa Claus contest. This one is the Easter contest. It's completely different. Start judging."

Michelle exchanged grins with Charles and Hugh. Then, all three got busy studying the pictures. Emma came in a little late and jumped right in. It was easy to see Emma loved this part of her job. They finally eliminated all but four pictures and were just trying to figure out places when Michelle's phone rang. She glanced at it and noticed a Little Rock number, so she stepped out to take the call.

"This is Michelle."

"Ms. Wilson, this is Officer McLennon. I'm investigating your car accident from a couple of weeks ago."

Her heart beat a little faster. Was there something he'd forgotten to ask? "Yes. I remember."

"I just wanted to touch base with you and give you an update. We figured out who the owner of the motorcycle is."

"Oh." Her breath came out in a whoosh. She wiped a sweaty palm on her pants.

"Unfortunately, his brother was driving it that night. The brother took off on the bike that afternoon, and the owner hasn't seen him since. We have several alerts out, and we're exploring all possibilities."

"Can't you just trace his cell phone or monitor his credit card?" She leaned against the table in the middle of the room.

"Regrettably, this isn't a television show, and it's not as easy as they make it look. It takes a bit longer than an hour, especially when the person doesn't keep a cell phone long and can't get a credit card because of bad credit."

"Oh." She didn't sound particularly intelligent right now.

"It's all right. We get questions like that a lot. TV has ruined our reputation in that way." His laughter echoed in her ear.

"Okay." She chewed on her bottom lip a moment. "But you're closer, right? You will catch him?"

"You bet. We got a new lead this morning, which we'll follow. I'll let you know as soon as we have him in custody, okay?"

"Thank you." She wasn't sure why it was such a big deal to her that this guy be apprehended, but it was. Instinct told her she'd be more comfortable driving when he was no longer on the road. And maybe it would help Kevin, too, to know that the man who'd killed his friends would no longer be able to do the same thing to someone else.

Michelle hung up, took a breath, and returned to the meeting. Hugh leaned against the door frame, his arms crossed. How long had he been there? Was he eavesdropping?

"The police with information about my wreck." Michelle held her phone up.

Hugh nodded. "I picked up on that."

"Did you guys need me in there?"

"Nah. We finished judging, and the bunnies have been put away for another year. Just coming to let you know the real part of the meeting is about to start."

Michelle nodded. "Okay. Well, I'm coming."

"I didn't realize your wreck was so bad that it required someone being chased down through cell phones and credit card records."

Michelle narrowed her eyes and tried to figure out how little she could get away with telling him.

"Sorry. Couldn't help overhearing. Hope they catch him soon." Hugh turned and went back to the conference room.

Michelle squared her shoulders and held her head up high as she followed. She would not let him get to her.

Dear Emma,

Michelle copied from the hand-written letter.

I know this is early, but it's come up now. My husband and I usually go to my parents' home for Thanksgiving and his parents' for Christmas. This year, his family wants us at Thanksgiving because of a relative's 80th birthday. My mom is fine with swapping, but his mom doesn't want to swap. She wants us for both holidays because she's never celebrated Christmas without my husband. How do I get out of this and make all of the parents happy?

Caught-in-the-Middle

Dear Caught-in-the-Middle,

You have to stand up for yourself. Point out to his mom that you will be going to see your family for one holiday or the other and then ask her to choose which one is more important for her to have you at her house. If she can't choose one, then decide for her. Don't let her ruin your holidays, though. If all else fails, go somewhere else for Christmas, and have both families meet you there.

Michelle hoped that would suffice as a good answer. Since she wasn't married, she had no experience trying to figure out with whom to spend holidays. She contemplated what it would be like to be in the letter writer's position but couldn't wrap her head around it. God willing, she would find someone to marry who'd be willing to live in Cedar Springs.

There she went again, making a mental list, an inventory of what she wanted in her future spouse. This situation with Grace had turned her thoughts toward matrimony more than ever. Up until now, she'd only had a vague impression of someday finding someone to marry. Now, it seemed more important.

But she had no idea where to begin finding someone to marry. She pretty much knew everyone in town, and every relationship she'd been in up until this point had ended after only a week or two.

She hit *save* on her computer and stopped herself from that line of thinking. God had someone out there for her. She just hadn't figured out who it was yet.

CHAPTER 11

"*H*appy Easter." Greg handed Michelle a plastic egg full of jellybeans as she came out of Bible class on Sunday morning. "Grace looks cute. I didn't know Kevin would be here today."

"Yeah, he decided last minute that he wanted to spend Easter morning with Grace." She tucked the treat into a side pocket on the diaper bag.

"Awkward or good?" Greg tried not to stare at the man holding the baby Michelle had her heart set on adopting. Could Kevin be attracted to Mickey's love for the child? He forced the jealousy away to focus on her answer.

"Not sure." Michelle shrugged. "I mean, I think he wants to be a part of her life but isn't certain how to go about it without seeming to just hang around. I think he's trying to find his balance. I get that. We're still trying to find a balance too."

"We haven't even talked since before he came last weekend. How did that go?" Greg walked with her toward the auditorium, hovering his hand over the small of her back. Not necessarily as if he were staking a claim, but if someone wanted to take it that way, he wouldn't fault them for it.

"It went very well. I even brought up my desire to adopt Grace."

Greg stopped, his heart speeding up, and faced her. "You did?"

"Yes. He said he'd pray about it." A wide smile spread across Michelle's face, bringing out that dimple to the right side of her lips he loved so much.

"Wow, Mickey. That's great." Greg couldn't insert enough enthusiasm into his voice to sound truly happy, but she didn't seem to notice.

"Yes, well, he didn't make any promises except that. But it's more than I was expecting, so it's a start."

Greg nodded.

Worship services would begin soon, and he was running out of time to accomplish what he'd set out to do when walking up to her this morning. He swallowed a few times, hoping his voice would start breaking like it had as a teenager. Now or never.

"Hey, are you going to Jessica's wedding next weekend?" That sounded nonchalant, right?

"I think I'd better since I'm the photographer." She smirked. "Why?"

"Oh, that's right! I forgot you were a professional photographer on the side. I was just wondering." His hands in his pockets, he ducked his head. It was ridiculous to be this nervous. "I mean, I'm one of the groomsmen, and we're supposed to have a date. I thought you might like to go with me."

"As a date?" Her expression said she'd rather date her brother.

Greg shrugged, his face heating. "Or 'plus one' if you'd prefer. But I guess it doesn't matter since you'll be busy the whole time."

"Sorry, Greg. You know how much I'd love to sit with you and make snide comments about the cheesiness factor, but

Jessica asked me to photograph it, and it's my first real step to getting my business up and running in this area."

"No worries." He squeezed her arm before he left her at the pew her family and Kevin had taken up and moved several rows forward to where his own family sat. No worries, indeed. Of all the ways he'd imagined that conversation going, the way it ended up fit none of them.

~

MICHELLE SAT DOWN WITH A FROWN. That was one of the weirdest conversations she'd ever had with Greg. What was going on in his head lately? She didn't have long to contemplate it because just then, her brother scooted in beside her with a crooked smile.

"Matt!"

"Surprise, Little Sis." He wiggled his eyebrows. His brown hair was long and his skin tan, but other than that, he looked pretty much like he always had, his hazel eyes twinkling with mischief.

"I didn't know you were coming home."

"Hence, the term *surprise*."

Michelle nudged him with her elbow. "Are you ever going to grow up?"

"Are you?"

She gave him a slight shove and then accepted Grace from Kevin's arms. "I want you to meet someone."

"This must be Grace." He reached over to touch the baby right as Grace released an enormous burp. "Oh, I see how it is. Just you wait, young lady. Uncle Matt will teach you how to do that even louder."

Michelle rolled her eyes but couldn't stifle the giggle that escaped.

"You two hush. It's time to start worship." Mom leaned forward to dictate her reprimand from the other side of Kevin.

Matt winked at Michelle, and she smothered a snicker. Hopefully, Mom wouldn't feel the need to come down and sit between them before the service was over.

She glanced up and met Greg's gaze from two rows ahead. He quickly looked back toward the front, but his ears were red. What was with him today? He surely hadn't meant to ask her on a date a few minutes ago. Not Greg. That would be like dating Matt.

"What's that face for?" Matt nudged her, and she realized she'd been grimacing.

"Nothing that concerns you."

"*Mm-hmm.* We'll talk more later."

Matt straightened as Mom shot them another look.

ON HOLIDAYS, the Marshalls and the Wilsons got together for lunch at one house or the other. Today was no exception. The savory smell of ham and potatoes and the sound of laughter filled Michelle's house. Everyone welcomed Kevin as if he were a member of both families. Soon, Matt and Phillip had him talking about sports and hunting. Darcy held Grace while Michelle helped make the salad and pour drinks.

"Are you sure you unlocked that side?" Dad grunted as he tugged on his end of Mom's antique table.

Greg and the dads were trying to add two extra leaves to the middle. But it took all three of them to pull it apart and then push it back together once it was extended. Sheila took the tablecloth and dishes to set the table while Mom finished the mashed potatoes.

Soon, everyone gathered around the table and held hands during the prayer. What did Kevin think of such a tradition? She glanced his direction, and he'd joined in the circle as well. Greg squeezed her hand on the right, and she returned the pressure. Maybe he'd act like his usual self for the rest of the day, and she wouldn't have to deal with the craziness that had enveloped their relationship lately.

After the prayer, it was every man for himself. Creamy spuds, rolls, ham, and green bean casserole made their way from hand to hand, with plenty for everyone. Greg snatched the bread away from Michelle before she could grab one, and she gave him a dirty look. He knew her mom's crescents were the best in town.

"You'd better hope there's still some in the basket when it gets back my way." She waved her butter knife at them.

"As if you could do anything with that thing." He popped a bite of roll in his mouth.

"Don't tempt me."

"You two quit flirting and pass the green beans." Matt nudged her arm.

Flirting!

For such audacity, he better be glad she didn't dump the green beans in his lap.

They finished off their meal with Sheila's Dreamsicle cake. Michelle savored each bite of the creamy orange dessert. Greg's finger slid over to her plate and swiped some icing from the edge.

"Seriously?"

She swatted at his hand, but he made it back to his mouth, unscathed.

"Can't we have one meal where you don't snitch something from my plate?"

"Only if we're not together." He smirked.

Grace was passed from adult to adult as the group finished the meal. Michelle cleared away the dishes. She hummed to herself as she loaded the dishwasher. Everyone else moved from their places at the table, sluggish and reluctant, as if in a food-induced coma. Darcy and Phillip announced they were going home to take a nap. Matt seemed to have the same idea as he stretched out in the recliner.

"Michelle, can I talk to you for a moment?" Kevin asked.

"Sure." She wiped her hands on a towel and followed him out to the back porch. The morning that began slightly chilly had quickly warmed up. She let the sunlight bathe her face for a moment.

Kevin waited for several moments before he said anything. "Your family is amazing. The Marshalls too. It's sort of what I imagined it would be like in the future for John's and my families."

"I'm so sorry, Kevin. I didn't realize how hard it was going to be on you."

"No. It's not that. I mean, that's not what I wanted to talk to you about." He sighed and hung his head. "I wanted to let you know that I kept my word, and I have been praying about what you told me last weekend. I've probably prayed about this more than I've ever prayed for anything in my entire life."

Michelle's heart rose in her chest. "And?"

"And I'm finding no peace about it. It's like, the thought of going against one of Leah and John's express wishes is just too much to bear. I can't let someone who isn't married adopt Grace."

Michelle couldn't speak.

"I'm sorry, Michelle, but I felt I needed to let you know now instead of later after you'd gotten your hopes up even more."

Numbness oozed through Michelle's body as if she'd been doused with an icy shower. She quickly tried to gather herself, blinked back the threatening tears, and managed to lift one corner of her mouth in a semi-smile as he turned to face her.

"I don't want you to do something you don't have peace about. But will you do me a favor?" Her voice squeaked as she finished her question.

"What's that?"

"Don't give up praying about it yet."

"Michelle—"

"Please, Kevin." She held her hand out but pulled back before actually touching him. "Just a little longer."

He nodded. "I better go. Things to do before work tomorrow."

As they turned back toward the house, Michelle noticed Greg standing halfway out onto the porch. He'd obviously heard the conversation but acted like he'd just opened the door.

Michelle held her emotions under control until after Kevin had bid everyone else goodbye and given his thanks to all. Then, she went straight to her room, sat in her little chair by the window, and let the tears fall.

∼

"Listen to this." Her mom shook the newspaper out later that day. "Dear Emma ..." She read out the letter Michelle had so carefully typed the other day at the office, along with Michelle's answer.

Her dad laughed. "She makes it sound rather easy, doesn't she? Remember that first year we were married and thought we had to hit every family member for at least two days? We were both miserable by the end of the trip."

"That's when we decided not to go anywhere for Christmas ever again. If they wanted to see us for the holidays, they could come to us." Her mom set the article aside.

"Maybe the person writing it has never had that exact experience." Michelle tried to sound nonchalant.

"Maybe. Then she should have asked someone else before writing the advice." Her mom took a sip of coffee.

"I didn't think it sounded that bad." Michelle played with the edge of the tablecloth. Her family had gathered around for an evening snack. The newspaper was spread out amongst the ones who didn't actually write for it.

"That's because you're an idealist." Matt looked up from the sports page. "One of the reasons we love you so much."

Grace cried from the other room, and Michelle rose to get the baby. She was glad for an excuse to leave. If they'd talked about her article one minute more, she might have spilled the truth about who really wrote it. She picked up the infant, another twinge hitting her heart as she realized she wouldn't get to take care of this little girl forever like she'd hoped.

For such a day of hope in most Christians' lives, this one hadn't turned out very happily for her. She'd been doing great until her talk with Kevin after lunch. If only she could go back and tell him she couldn't talk right then. Maybe never. Could he have changed his mind before talking to her if she'd put him off today?

GREG WASN'T SUPPOSED to have heard the conversation between Kevin and Michelle earlier. He should just put it from his mind. Block it completely. Gone forever.

If only it were that easy.

The only reason he'd followed them out was jealousy, pure and simple. When he'd see them go off by themselves, all he could think about was the earlier thought of wondering if Kevin were interested in Michelle. He hadn't expected to hear Kevin crush her dreams.

Yet, they'd been crushed. She'd tried to hide it, but he'd known her for too long. Had he tried to comfort her? No. He pretended like he didn't know.

But he did.

And she knew it, too.

"What am I supposed to do?"

His cat offered no reply. Useless beast.

Seeing her complete disappointment changed his mind for the first time through this whole thing. Up to now, he'd had his doubts about her adopting Grace. But he couldn't stand her being heartbroken.

She needed a husband.

"A husband."

There was no way he could stand back and watch her marry someone else.

"No way."

So, finding her someone else wasn't an option.

He paced the kitchen floor as he worked through the situation. The cat's eyes followed him, her tail twitching off beat. Why had he wanted that animal again?

"Focus." He held up a finger. "She needs a husband. She's not dating anyone. So, who can she marry?"

Qualifications of a husband?

"A man." Absolutely.

He stopped. Wasn't there a Christmas movie that said almost that same thing?

"Focus."

Okay. She needed a man. Helpful if she knew him, although supposedly people married strangers in other parts of the world. He couldn't imagine that working out easily. Besides, he'd already decided he didn't want her to marry anyone else.

And that brought him back to square one.

"If she can't marry anyone else, she has to marry me or stay unmarried and lose Grace."

Deep inside, he'd known he was headed to that deduction, but it still stopped him in his tracks.

It would never work. No way would she go for such a plan.

He'd have to keep thinking. *God, a little wisdom here would be nice.* He shook his head. *Or maybe even a lot.*

∾

JUST AS MICHELLE HAD FIGURED, her father had been quietly searching websites and car lots to find her the perfect replacement vehicle. Thursday evening, he took her to see what he'd found. The first three places didn't have anything she was interested in, but the fourth had a perfect little blue crossover.

She liked the fact it was small like a sedan but with more cargo room.

Her dad helped her work out the paperwork, and she followed him home. The sun was just setting, and she pulled the visor down to block some of the sunset's glare. They wove through the old-fashioned downtown area that still had a drug store complete with a soda fountain. She glanced in the windows of the second-hand dress shop to see if they had anything of interest. Then, three more blocks to the house.

She pulled into her familiar spot in front of the basketball goal and turned the car off. It was her third vehicle but probably her favorite so far, with seat warmers and a CD player. She clicked the button on her key fob and locked it. Now, she just had to work up the bravery to drive at night again.

CHAPTER 12

"*Y*ou look nice." Mom stuck her head into her room on Saturday afternoon.

"Thanks. I figured a pantsuit would work better for photographing Jessica's wedding than a dress. Do you think she'll care?" Michelle blinked against a mascara wand.

"I think she'll be so focused on getting married to Simon that she won't notice what anyone else is wearing." Mom leaned against the doorframe. "Who's keeping Grace tonight?"

Michelle turned from finishing her makeup and looked at her mother. She had on a nice dress and had her hair fixed as if she were going out.

"I thought you and Dad were." Michelle screwed the mascara tube closed.

"Oh, Honey. We have to go to a thing your dad's company is putting on. No kids allowed. The invitation has been on the fridge for weeks now. I thought you'd seen it."

"I guess I didn't pay much attention to the actual date." A tingle of worry worked its way up her back.

"Well, you'll come up with something."

Michelle put her hands on her hips. "Mom, there's no way I can take Grace. I have to be all over the place, taking pictures."

"You were the one who wanted the responsibility of having a baby. You wanted to be a parent. This is part of it. Taking care of all the details, not just getting up in the middle of the night. Sometimes, having kids gets in the way of your plans." Her mother spread her hands as if in apology.

Michelle bit back a retort that would only make her sound like a spoiled brat. Mom was right, but that didn't mean she appreciated her mother pointing it out right now.

"I thought the deal about acting like she's mine was only good until there was no more hope that she would be mine."

"We can discuss that later, but I'm not changing my mind. You've known about this event for months. We assumed you'd lined up a sitter." Mom sliced her hand through the air. "There's no way your father and I can get out of going to this. His job, well, never mind, but suffice it to say, we need to go."

"There's no way I can find someone who'd be approved by the state agency so quickly. I have to leave in ten minutes."

Whatever Mom was about to say was interrupted when Dad called her from the other room.

She gave her a maybe-this-is-why-you-shouldn't-be-a-parent-yet look, then kissed Michelle's forehead. "Time to prove you can do what you said you could—and I know you can. Love you."

Mom was gone in a waft of perfume before Michelle could even reply. She stomped her foot on the carpet and growled. What could she do?

Grabbing the diaper bag, she made sure it was packed, added a few bottles and formula, and then searched through Grace's room to find the baby carrier, which would allow Michelle to wear Grace strapped to her front. She started to put the baby in the pouch and then remembered that first, she needed to be in the car seat. Michelle lugged all her equipment out to the car and then hauled all Grace's things.

"Okay, Gracie. You get to help Mommy tonight. That means no crying, okay?"

Once she had them both buckled in, she backed out of the

driveway and headed to the church building, hoping she wasn't late. Her foot waged war on the gas pedal, wanting to speed up, but also knowing to drive safely, considering the precious cargo in the backseat.

Jessica had already had her portraits made, so today they were just doing behind the scenes shots and group photos before the ceremony. Michelle strapped on the carrier, looped all her bags over her shoulder, and somehow managed to situate Grace into the pouch. She took a deep breath and headed inside.

Michelle wound her way through the foyer into the ladies' room down the classroom hallway. Jessica was there with her bridesmaids, putting on finishing touches of makeup and hairspray.

"Freeze, ladies. Let me get a few pictures." Michelle snapped a few candid shots of the girls getting ready. "Beautiful."

Then, she set up her equipment in the auditorium for a few group shots before guests arrived. Grace slept soundly in her carrier, and Michelle released a breath of tension. *Thank you, God, for this small favor.*

The matron-of-honor led the party into the auditorium. "I can't wait to see his face when he first sees you in this dress, Jess. His eyes may fall out of his head."

"That dress is perfect on you." Another bridesmaid chimed in, lifting her skirt to climb the stairs.

"Of course, he'd think you're beautiful in a burlap sack. He's so in love." Jessica's sister playfully nudged the bride with her bouquet.

Michelle grouped the girls into several different poses that she and Jessica had discussed beforehand. Then, they closed off the room and brought in Simon for his first peek at his bride. Michelle zoomed in and caught several great shots of the intimate moment. This was her favorite part of shooting weddings. She hoped someday to find a man who would react that way when he saw her in a wedding gown.

The rest of the wedding party burst in and interrupted, and

Michelle prepared to do the rest of the pictures quickly so they could clear out and allow guests to come in. Most people would probably pay more attention to the gorgeous bride or the look of complete joy on the groom's face. But this photographer was having a lot of trouble keeping her attention off of a certain groomsman.

When had Greg started to look so handsome? It was probably just the tuxedo. Fancy clothes tended to turn a girl's head.

Near the end of the group shots, Grace started to stir. Michelle bounced a little while she directed everyone where to stand, pausing only to snap the photos. She finished the last two arrangements and motioned them to return to their dressing rooms to wait.

"Why isn't she with Lisa and Bryce?" Greg asked.

Michelle came down from the stage. "They had a dinner for Dad's job tonight. I didn't even think about it until it was too late to line up a sitter. I'll just have to make do."

"Darcy and Phillip are coming. Why don't we get her to take care of Grace?"

"Greg, I can't always just go pass her off to your sister. That's not fair."

"What if she were to start crying right in the middle of the ceremony? You couldn't just take her out. You have to do something."

Grace started fussing at that moment as if just to prove his point.

"Do you always have to be right?"

"Just ninety-nine-point nine percent of the time."

He pulled his phone out and texted his sister. Ten minutes later, Darcy had the diaper bag and baby in hand, and Michelle was free to move about as she needed.

"I'll make it up to you." Michelle readjusted her camera strap now that it didn't have to stretch over a baby's head.

Darcy waved her off.

The ceremony was beautiful. Everything was simple but elegant, just perfect for Jessica and her groom. The words of the preacher fell over Michelle as she snapped photos from various angles, trying to stay out of the way of the other guests.

"Marriage is not to be taken lightly. This is a pact you're making not only with each other but also with God. I know you're both Christians, and that you consider God to be first in your lives. But I want you to make sure He's first in your marriage too. Jesus said, 'What God has joined together, let not man separate.'"

Michelle thought about several married couples she knew, including her parents and grandparents. It was apparent God influenced their decisions and actions. Her parents didn't always agree on everything—like when Mom said Michelle could get her ears pierced at age thirteen, and Dad thought that was still too young—but they always worked things out calmly.

Even if it meant one of them conceding to the other and letting Michelle get earrings. And she'd seen them having private Bible studies more than once early in the mornings.

"I, Jessica Glass, promise to love and obey you in sickness and health."

Jessica had been one of Michelle's other best friends in high school. They hadn't shared as much as she and Greg, but they'd still been close and kept up online after Michelle moved away. Jessica was thrilled when she found out Michelle would be back in the area in time to photograph her wedding.

Michelle thought back to a youth retreat they'd all gone on in the eleventh grade. The speaker had held a mock wedding ceremony to remind them that not only would they marry a man or woman when they grew up, but also, and more importantly, they were married to God when they became Christians.

As part of the church, they were members of Christ's bride. She hadn't thought about that in years, but it now hit her—she hadn't been living her life as if God were her husband.

When Jessica and Simon shared their first kiss as man and

wife, Michelle snapped photos, but she also prayed. She asked God to help her put Him back in first place in her life and strive more to meet His wants than her own. Grace's fussy noises echoed a bit in the back of the room and reminded Michelle it wouldn't be easy. Because she still wanted Grace to be her own too.

~

MAYBE IT WAS the fact that they were at a wedding. Maybe it was all the old emotions unearthed now that they were once again living in the same town. For whatever reason, Greg couldn't keep his eyes off Michelle. Or his mind away from the idea he formed earlier.

It was the craziest, most hare-brained scheme he'd ever come up with. Or maybe proposal would be a better term for it. Because despite everything, more than anything, he wanted Michelle to be happy.

And she had her heart set on being Grace's mother.

God, help me here. Is this wrong? Is it somehow sinful? Because I can't block it from my mind now.

'Marriage is not to be taken lightly. This is a pact you're making not only with each other but also with God.' The preacher's words from earlier echoed in his heart.

If that was God's answer, Greg might be in trouble.

No.

He wasn't doing anything lightly. And he'd keep his vows if this worked. That part would be easy.

After all, he'd mean every word of promising to love and cherish for the rest of his life. It's what he'd longed for forever.

But would she go for it?

God, how do I do this?

When he'd considered proposing to Michelle in the past, he'd always planned out an elaborate situation complete with fancy dinner or candles or starlight or anything else romantic women always seemed to drool over in the movies. But Michelle's time with Grace might be running out, and she needed a solution sooner rather than later. No time to plan. Only act.

"You may now kiss the bride."

Michelle's finger moved rapidly as she captured the scene through her lens, working to get the best angle. As she pulled the camera away from her eye, he caught her gaze, and time froze for several breaths. She licked her lips, gave a little grin, and then went back to work, memorializing someone else's special day.

Would they be able to have a wedding so fancy, or would it need to be simpler for the adoption paperwork to proceed quickly? Would she even agree to his plan?

It would be a dream-come-true for him, but could she see it in such a light?

Only one way to find out.

GREG'S HEART hammered as he slid into a seat next to Michelle near the end of the wedding reception. "Are you finished?"

"Until the bride and groom get ready to leave, I'm mostly off duty. I already snapped shots of the cakes, garter, and bouquet. And I caught several cute shots of the flower girls spinning on the dance floor too."

"It was nice, huh?" Greg propped his chin on his fist.

"It was beautiful. Made me think a lot."

"Oh?" Had her mind gone the way of his after all?

"Remember that youth retreat all those years ago where we had that mock wedding ceremony and promised our lives to God?"

Okay. Not the same direction at all.

Greg sat back and crossed his arms. "Yeah."

"I hadn't thought about it in years, but it's really on my heart tonight, seeing all this."

"That's not what I expected you to think about while seeing this wedding. But if it's where your mind went, then I'm sure God had a reason."

"Whatever that means." Michelle flicked a peanut at him.

"I've been doing some thinking this week too."

"Sounds dangerous." She smirked.

"It probably is, but I think if I don't say this, I may not get up the nerve again." He studied his hands as he scooped up and scattered the confetti on the table.

Michelle raised an eyebrow. "Spill it."

"The reason Kevin won't let you adopt Grace is because you're not married, right?" He glanced up.

"That's probably the main reason, yes." She frowned. "Why?"

Greg took a deep breath, willing steel to his backbone and strength to his lungs to get the words out. "Okay. So, let's get married."

Michelle almost fell out of her chair. "Are you insane?"

He should have expected that reaction. Maybe even had, in all reality. Hadn't that been one of the million scenarios he'd played out in his head over the last six days?

It didn't stop it from feeling like a stab wound. He'd gone this far. Might as well give her the opportunity to drive the blade in farther—time to play to her love of facts.

"It makes sense. I mean, neither one of us is interested in anyone else, we get along okay, and you need a husband to be able to give Grace both a mommy and a daddy. It gets you what you want, right?"

"I'd drive you crazy." She scooted a bit further away. "Please don't joke about this."

"I'm not joking, Michelle."

He didn't use her nickname—something he only did when he was serious. A gleam of insanity flitted through her eyes as if she'd like to throw a fit. But she'd never cause a scene in front of all these people—one of the reasons he'd chosen to go ahead and do this tonight.

"It would never work." She shook her head.

"Why not?"

She opened and closed her mouth about three times. "You're like a brother to me."

"You lived with Matt for almost sixteen years and never killed him."

"Seriously?" She leaned forward and lowered her voice. "What if you find someone else you really would rather be married to a few years down the road? You'd be stuck with Grace and me. It wouldn't be fair to either one of us."

Greg shook his head. "I wouldn't even look."

"What if I found someone else?"

That was unexpected. And low. The knife had to be in past the hilt now. It hurt even worse than her calling him insane or a brother.

He looked down at the table, where he'd annihilated one of the fancy napkins. What else could he say to convince her? Too late. Darcy showed up right then.

"She's getting pretty sleepy. I texted your mom, and they're home now. Why don't we take her on to the house, and then you can go home when you're done here?" Darcy held the baby as if it were the most natural thing in the world.

Grace's head bobbed a bit to the left as her eyes drooped. Michelle nodded and reached for the diaper bag. She searched the pockets with shaky fingers, maybe looking for keys.

"I'll just help you get the car seat moved."

Greg squeezed her arm. "Why not let Darcy take your car and Phillip follow her? That car seat isn't easy to move from vehicle to vehicle, and that way they can go now." And that would give him a few more minutes to make his argument.

"It would leave me stranded." Michelle tried a different pocket.

"I won't make you walk home." Greg's voice brokered no argument. "I'll give you a ride."

Michelle held out the keys and bag. "It's the new little blue Ford in the parking lot on the west side of the building."

~

AFTER DARCY AND PHILLIP LEFT, the wedding festivities wrapped up quickly. Michelle snapped a few pictures of the decorated car as it pulled away, and she was officially done. She followed Greg back into the building, uncomfortable around her best friend for the first time in her life. Their earlier conversation ran through her head again and again while she waited in the foyer for him to change out of his tuxedo.

She wanted to wring Greg's neck. Why could he not see that this was the stupidest idea he'd ever suggested? And he said she was the one who made crazy plans. Why would he even put this possibility in her head?

He picked up her camera bag and walked on through the foyer. As she followed him out into the dark, realization struck, he'd saved her from facing her fear of driving in the dark. Had that been part of his intention in suggesting this? She slid into the passenger seat and pulled her seatbelt tight.

"You okay?" He paused before turning the ignition.

"No." How could she be?

Nothing was said for the short trip to her house. He pulled in the driveway and parked behind her new car. The front light was on for her. She didn't remember turning it on, so she figured her parents had flipped it on when they got home.

"We didn't finish our conversation." He leaned against his door.

"The insane one we were having earlier?"

"Yes."

"Greg, you're not thinking this through." She picked at a spot on her cast where the cotton frayed. "Why are you even suggesting marrying someone who doesn't love you like that? What do you get out of this?"

"I get to see you happy. I get to be Grace's daddy. I won't have to wonder if I'll ever find someone who will marry me. I won't have to cook for myself or always be the one doing the laundry." He ticked the reasons off like a grocery list.

"You want a maid, not a wife."

"Pretty sure me getting a maid wouldn't help make you happy."

"It would if it got this crazy idea out of your head. Greg, please, stop this. I've missed you for the last few years and was looking forward to having you around again. Please don't ruin it for me. This won't work."

She got out of the Jeep before he could reply and clomped up the gravel driveway in her high heels.

"Mickey!"

She turned and saw Greg coming after her with her camera bag in hand.

"Thought you might need this. I'm sure Jessica will want pictures when she gets back from Jamaica." He gently looped it over her shoulder.

Michelle nodded.

"Good night, Mick." He kissed her forehead, and when he leaned back, something flickered in his eyes—a look that seemed to hold more than friendship.

"Good night."

She went inside, ignoring her parents in the living room, and headed straight to bed. Eventually, she and her mom would have to talk about their earlier conversation, but not now. She'd thought her prayer to ask God to help her put Him first in her life would make things easier. Instead, a whole new set of issues popped up. And the problem was, somewhere in the back of her mind, she was actually considering taking Greg up on his offer.

CHAPTER 13

"There's some sort of protest going on out at the greeting card factory." Emma's voice cut through Michelle's private thoughts halfway through their Tuesday morning meeting.

At Dad's job? What had Mom said the other night when they were getting ready to leave? She had to get out there and check on him.

"I'll cover it," Michelle and Hugh said at the same time.

The following stare-off was almost deadly in its intensity. Michelle, on one side of the table. Hugh on the other. Did anyone else hear the Western movie music playing in the background? Michelle stopped herself before patting her hip in search of a gun to draw. Emma cleared her throat where she stood at the end.

"My Dad works out there." Michelle pointed out the window. "I can probably get in and get their side of the story as well as those protesting."

Hugh's jaw visibly clenched and unclenched. "But wouldn't that make you biased?"

"Why don't you both cover it?" Emma leaned over the table to get between them. "One on the inside and one on the out."

Michelle and Hugh exchanged another menacing glance, and then both nodded.

The team divvied up the rest of the assignments—the teacher/student volleyball game at the high school, the preparations for the 100th Annual Cotton Festival later that summer, the monthly meeting of the Garden Society, and the oldest member of the town turning a hundred and one.

Had it already been a month since Michelle started working here? It didn't seem that long, but at the same time, it was like she'd been here forever. She had never been as comfortable in the two years she worked in Little Rock as she was here after just four weeks.

"Want to go check out the protest?" Hugh glanced through messages on his phone as they headed back to their cubicles.

"Sure. Let me grab my camera."

He rolled his eyes. "What's wrong with the camera on your phone?"

"Nothing." She draped the strap over her head. "This one just gets better shots. I can catch more details and action by using different shutter speeds and lenses."

"That went right over my head."

"Not surprising." Her snarky tone of voice wasn't as Christ-like as it probably should have been, but she couldn't completely change in a month. "It took several classes for me to figure it all out," she added.

Out in the parking lot, she headed to her car without thinking, only to realize halfway there that he'd headed for his truck. They stopped and looked at each other again.

He held up his keys and clicked the unlock button. "I'll drive."

"I can drive, too, you know." She placed her hands on her hips.

"Yeah, but you've been in at least one more wreck than I have. I like my odds better than yours."

She bit her tongue. He was making it hard for her to take her mom's advice to quit thinking of him on her gotta-get-even-with-him list. She climbed into his passenger seat after pushing several papers and receipts out of the way. He obviously lived in his vehicle.

"Sorry about the mess." He dropped a few more papers behind his seat.

"Your odds would have been better in that area in my car." She passed him three empty fast food cups.

"Oh, well." He revved his engine and headed north toward the card factory.

Michelle tried to think of anything her dad might have said that would indicate a reason for all this. She couldn't recall a single mention of problems brewing out here. Of course, she had to admit she'd thought of nothing but what Greg had proposed —literally—since Saturday night.

On Sunday, he'd acted like nothing had changed, and she tried to play along since she was the one who requested they go back to the way they were in high school. But it hadn't been easy. Every time she opened her mouth, she wanted to bring it up again.

"Has much changed since you left?" Hugh interrupted her thoughts.

Greg lost his mind. She gave herself a mental shake. Hugh meant the town in general.

She shrugged. "Maybe a little. But that's one of the reasons I wanted to move back in the first place. I like the fact that nothing changes here. It's comfortable."

"Comfortable like a worn-out shoe that needs replacing because the water leaks through the soles."

"Wow." She leaned back in her seat. "I figured you loved it here. Isn't that why you took the job two years ago?"

"I took the job because my family told me I had to at least start at the family paper." He glanced over at her.

"I never knew. I mean, I always supposed part of the reason

you got it was because you were family, but I never knew how you felt about it."

"Assuming things is a dangerous business for a newspaper writer." He hit the turn signal with a bit more force than necessary. "Facts tend to work a lot better for figuring things out."

Michelle nodded.

"I see you and Greg picked up right where you left off."

"Best friends forever." The words almost choked her. At least they'd kept their insane conversation a secret from the rest of the town.

"Still sticking to that old story, huh?" Hugh huffed as he caught up with a tractor with no way to pass.

"What's that supposed to mean?"

"Everyone in high school assumed you two would end up married long before now." He started to pull around the John Deere, only to swerve back into their lane. A minivan flew past seconds later. "Why do you think those relationships you had in high school were so short? The guys said even when Greg was nowhere around, they still didn't have you away from him. He was all you ever talked about."

Michelle realized her mouth was hanging open. "If they couldn't accept my friendship with Greg, it's best we broke up anyway." Everyone expected them to get married? What was it with everyone all of a sudden? First Greg, and now Hugh, bringing up the *M-word* as if it were fate.

"I think you just don't want to admit that you've got something more with Greg than friendship."

She folded her arms across her chest. "Guys and girls can be friends without including romance."

"Wasn't there a character in a popular movie who spouted that same line? Before they ended up getting married."

Michelle couldn't win for losing. Time for a subject change. "What about you and Vanessa? How did that happen?"

"We never really left town." He finally made it past the farm equipment and picked up speed again. "We came back right after college. When you do that, you've got to find someone else in town to have a relationship with. We started hanging out some. Turned into a few dates. She started dragging me to church. You know. The usual small-town story."

"That doesn't sound like you even like her."

"I do like her. I like her enough that if you look in that glove compartment, you'll find a little black box with a diamond ring in it. I just haven't figured out when I'm going to ask her yet."

Speechless, Michelle was grateful they'd reached the card factory. Cars lined either side of the street, and they pulled over and parked behind the last one. As they approached the gate, the chanting of people increased in volume, but not enough to understand what they were saying.

Michelle stopped and snapped a few photos of various people wielding their signs. Hugh waited beside her, his presence, surprisingly, adding a sense of security when surrounded by so many angry faces.

"You sure you can get through there to talk to your dad?" Hugh yelled over the screaming protestors.

"There's got to be a way. I will text him and see if he has any ideas."

Dad replied for her to come around to the back of the factory so he could meet her there. Hugh motioned her to the truck, and they cut through a subdivision until they reached the rear gate. Dad stood there with the security man. Evidently, none of the protestors thought about this entrance because all was quiet here.

"What are you doing here?" Dad pulled her into a hug.

"Just trying to do my job. We've got to go where the stories are."

"Not if they're dangerous." He chucked her under the chin.

"I'm not a little girl anymore."

"No. I guess you're not." He turned to Hugh and shook his hand.

"So, can you tell us anything? We saw the signs, but they don't make sense. *Don't be a sell-out! Locals before Greed!* What's going on?" Michelle held up her camera so he could see the view screen.

Dad ran his hands through his hair. Was it grayer than it had been a few days before?

"The owner is talking about selling the company. Southern Wishes is interested in buying but aren't sure they want to keep the factory here. They think they have a better location."

"But that would take away all these jobs." Michelle waved her hands to encompass the area. "It would kill the town."

"The company is dying as it is right now." Dad shrugged. "The owner has to do something, and he thinks this may be the best way."

"I'll go interview some of the people out front." Hugh touched her arm. "I'll come back here in about an hour or so. Sound good?"

"Sure." Michelle nodded. She walked with Dad up to his office.

The factory still ran, but not at full capacity. At least half of their workers were out front protesting. The familiar scent of paper surrounded her, reminding her of past visits growing up. A lot of people thought the smell was unpleasant, but to her, it meant a job for Dad, and she didn't consider it repulsive.

"How did this happen? It's like everything in Cedar Springs is going crazy." She leaned against the edge of his desk. "The newspaper is barely bringing in enough money to pay all the writers and keep the lights on. Your company is looking to sell. What's happening to my hometown?"

"Not everything stays the same." Dad eased into his chair. "The way things are right now, if we don't sell out, half those people down there won't have a job anyway because we'll have to lay them off. They think they're protecting their jobs, but they might lose them no matter what."

"Isn't there anything we can do? I mean, there has to be a solution." She tapped her pen against the edge of her notebook.

"I don't know. My hands are pretty much tied." He straightened a stack of papers on his blotter.

"Why is the business going down so much? Is there something that can be fixed?"

"People don't send mail like they used to. When they don't send mail, it means they don't need to buy greeting cards." He pointed to a chart standing nearby. "The price has gone up. You used to be able to buy a card for barely anything, and now the best ones cost at least four dollars. Add that to the crazy price for shipping, and it just doesn't add up like it used to."

"But you're one of the guys who markets this. Isn't there something you can do?"

"I'm not Superman. I can't go out and make people buy greeting cards. I can only advertise it in a way that makes it sound like a good idea." He leaned back again. "Maybe I'm not that good at marketing anymore."

"Dad ..." Her heart broke, seeing him like this. It was probably the first time she'd ever seen her father doubt.

She made a few more notes and let the conversation drift to unimportant things until Hugh texted he was at the back gate.

Michelle sat quietly on the ride back with Hugh. He said he got some good quotes. She had a few, too, but she wasn't sure how to write this with an unbiased perspective. This was Dad's job, and a third of the town's as well. There had to be a way to make things better.

THAT NIGHT, the same dream haunted her as it had again and again over the last month. She was driving at night and nearing the intersection. This time, she knew what was going to happen and braced herself as the motorcycle zipped through. The truck hit her, and she felt every jerk of her body as the airbag exploded, and her car spun to a stop. She got out on shaky legs and ran to the truck.

It stood upside down, the tires still spinning. John was climbing out of his window. He moaned and motioned to the passenger side of the car, but Michelle knew Leah wouldn't be there. The hole in the windshield was testimony to the fact that Leah had flown through. Michelle scanned the area until she saw a woman's form slumped a few feet farther up the road. She rushed to her side.

"Leah, can you hear me?" Michelle screamed.

Sirens wailed in the distance even though she hadn't called the police yet in this dream. Leah's eyes fluttered open, and her hands covered her pregnant belly. A tear ran down her cheek.

"Grace," Leah whispered.

"I've got her, Leah. I'm taking care of her for you." Michelle tenderly ran a hand down Leah's arm.

Leah reached out and grasped Michelle's hand. "Save my baby. Save Grace."

Michelle sat up in her bed, heart pounding in her chest. Mom held her hand, a worried expression on her face as Michelle heaved in a deep breath.

Mom brushed Michelle's hair back and put her other hand on Michelle's shoulder. "You okay? I heard you shouting."

"It was the dream again." Michelle rubbed her eyes. "A little different."

"You said Leah's name."

Michelle nodded. "This time, I went over to her, and she told me to save Grace."

"Honey, we're doing all we can. Grace is going to be fine."

"No, Mom. Not everything."

CHAPTER 14

"Michelle, this is Diana, the caseworker for Grace."

Michelle held her phone closer to her ear and looked around to make sure no one else was paying any attention to her. Her lunch break was almost over, and she was the only one in the parking lot at the moment.

"Yes, Diana. How are you?"

"I'm doing well, thanks. I just wanted to see if it would be possible for Kevin and me to bring a couple by this weekend. They seem promising, and they wanted to meet Grace."

Michelle forced herself not to glance down and see if her heart really had hit the pavement. She hadn't yet had time to come up with a plan to follow dream-Leah's admonition. She needed longer. She sucked in a breath and made her voice sound as cheery as possible.

"Of course. What time should we expect you?"

After working out the details, Michelle wandered into the office and stashed her purse. She and Hugh had moved to the conference table in the middle of the room so they'd be able to share notes and spread out. She grabbed a pencil and flopped back into the chair she'd been using, staring blankly at the piece of paper she'd written on earlier.

How was she supposed to focus on this when Grace's future hung in the balance? At some point, Hugh returned and got to work. But her focus was almost impossible to reign in.

"Hey." Hugh snapped his fingers in front of Michelle's face. "Earth to Michelle. You can't solve this. It's not your job. Our job is to report the facts. Period. Get rid of the emotions, and write the facts."

They spread their interview notes out on the long table. She flipped through photos she'd taken while there and hadn't even realized she'd tuned him out—or that he'd been talking in the first place.

"I know that in my head. It's just really hard."

"Yes, well, that's why not everyone can do our job. You're the one who wanted to move back to a town where you have a history. That makes writing stories like this harder. It's personal. Pretend like this is in Little Rock, and write it the way you would if that were true. It's okay to appeal to people's emotions some in the paper, but our job is to present facts. Make a list of facts." He pushed a pad of paper and a pen in her direction.

She took the pen and tapped it against the notebook, then made a bullet point and wrote *company wants to move factory to another town*. Under that, she made an arrow and wrote out the reasons why it would benefit the company. She added another dot and wrote down why the owner of the factory might sell out in the first place.

Scanning the list of numbers her dad had given her, she agreed, something needed to change, or the plant would die no matter what.

"Instead of doing it as one article, it needs to be two. Two articles on the same subject and go together, but from different viewpoints." Michelle stood. "I can't write here. I do better when I'm typing."

Hugh nodded as he scribbled on his own pad of paper. She grabbed her notes and marched back to her cubicle. A new word processor document shone on her computer screen, just waiting for her to add the first words.

A fixture in this town for over twenty years, she typed, *Greetings from Arkansas, our local greeting card factory, may not grace the town of Cedar Springs much longer.*

She told about the lower sales, the rising price of postage, the higher costs of manufacturing. Then, she added a quote she got from the owner.

'I don't want to sell the company. She's been a part of my family and this town for a long time. Unfortunately, I don't see many other options. I'm not sure yet what I'll do, but selling is looking like the best option for everyone.'

She wrapped up by giving more details about Southern Wishes wanting to buy them out. She gave the reasons they hoped to move the factory south of Cedar Springs, mainly to be closer to the interstate to reduce shipping costs. She summed up the piece by describing the compensation packages the new company planned to give to each family affected by the sale.

Michelle skimmed over each paragraph again. This absolutely had to be her best work. She also wanted to make sure it was as unbiased as she could make it.

"Looks good." Hugh's voice came from right over her shoulder.

She jumped and turned to look at him. "How long have you been there?"

"Long enough to read what you wrote. When I couldn't hear you typing anymore, I figured you were finished and thought you'd want to trade and make sure my article meshed with yours."

Michelle started to agree to a swap, then paused. Even though they started their day at odds with each other, Hugh had done nothing but help her make this article the best it could be, even making sure she was safe from the protestors. Maybe it was time to follow Greg's advice and give the guy a chance.

"I trust you."

Hugh lifted an eyebrow and then nodded. "Okay."

⁓

GREG WOULD SEE MICHELLE TONIGHT, right after Wednesday evening Bible study. Sunday had been awkward. And they hadn't had time to talk since then because she'd been swamped with the greeting card factory mess.

It wasn't that Greg wished away his proposal. Maybe wished it had gone more smoothly.

Had she given it more thought?

"Hey, GM." Trevor gave a fist bump as he slumped through the door of Bible class. "What's up?"

"Not much, man. How's baseball going?" Greg forced his thoughts back to the here and now. The last thing he needed was to accidentally mention anything about his personal life during a lesson to a bunch of teenagers. They gossiped more than the widow group.

"We're 6-0 for the season." Trevor pumped his arm in the air before moving on to join some of the other guys.

Another girl, one of the quieter ones, slipped through the door. "You okay, Mr. Greg? You look a little upset."

"Fine, Casey. Thanks for checking on me, though."

Her cheeks blushed pink as she ducked her head. "You're welcome."

Huh? Maybe Michelle wasn't so far off from her guess that all the teenage girls were in love with him. Yet another positive that would come if she'd agree to his proposal. The girls would have to give up their crushes and dreams.

As he called the class to attention and glanced down at where they left off the week before, he stifled a grimace. Why, of all the chapters in 1 Corinthians, did they have to be on the love chapter this week? And how had he not foreseen this when he was studying for it on Monday?

"First Corinthians, chapter thirteen. Let's get into the Word."

While they sorted through the verses, discussing why so many people used them for wedding ceremonies and how they could be used in other parts of life, Greg kept a mental list going of how it applied to his situation.

Patient, kind, not envious or boastful.

Sure. He had those down toward Michelle, right?

Not arrogant or rude. Didn't insist on its own way.

Eh. Mostly when they acted like that, they were playing.

Not irritable or resentful.

That one was a bit harder lately.

Doesn't rejoice in wrong. Rejoices in the truth.

Easy enough.

Bears all things, believes all things, hopes all things, endures all things. Love never fails.

Could he bear all things if Michelle didn't agree to this —ever?

The words reverberated through his thoughts as he left class and searched for the one who was never far from his mind. Not in the building. There. Going through the doors to the parking lot. And looking like the weight of the world rested on her shoulders.

God, help me lift some of her weight.

"What's wrong?" Greg appeared next to her car after Bible class.

Michelle looked up from buckling Grace into her car seat. "The caseworker is coming this weekend. Wants to bring a couple by to meet Grace."

"You knew this would happen sooner or later." He leaned against her car. "Babies don't stay unadopted for very long."

"Greg, you're not helping, okay?" She slammed the door harder than she meant to.

He held up his hands. "Sorry. I don't guess you've changed your mind, but I just wanted to let you know that my offer still stands."

Michelle didn't answer. What could she say? Obviously, we should get married, Greg. The whole town has been expecting it our entire lives. *And it's the only way I'll get to keep Grace.* Let's elope.

No. There had to be another way.

"I can't do this right now, Greg. I'll see you later." She climbed in the car without even saying bye.

Back at her parents' house, she changed Grace into pajamas, then sat in the rocker and fed the baby a bottle. She hadn't bothered to turn on anything but the nightlight. Her parents were discussing something in another room, but Michelle wasn't in the mood to talk with them. They knew the possible family was coming this weekend, and they seemed glad about it. She couldn't face that.

Grace's big, blue eyes were still wide awake. Michelle brushed her good hand over the baby's soft skin. Grace reached out and caught Michelle's finger in her tiny little hand. It might as well have been Michelle's heart—the squeeze in her chest was a like a vice, restricting the normal rhythm of its beating. How could she let Grace go forever? How could she let John and Leah down?

"What are we going to do, Little Girl? How can I fulfill your mama's wishes from my dream, as well as your mama's wishes from her will? Which wishes do you think matter most?"

Maybe she could just take Grace and run away. Surely there was somewhere in the country they wouldn't be found. Perhaps they could go to Alaska, or somewhere you couldn't get to by car. She shook that crazy thought from her head. That was even more insane than actually considering marrying Greg.

"What do you think? Which sounds better? Daddy? Or Uncle Greg?"

Grace just stared up at Michelle.

"Yeah. I don't know, either."

"DOES SHE NORMALLY CRY THIS MUCH?" Diana asked as she held Grace on Saturday. She and Kevin stood in the kitchen while they all waited for the possible parents to arrive.

"It's one of her bad days. She gets a bit colicky at times. The doctor said it's nothing to worry about long-term. She doesn't do it all the time, but some days, you just can't get her to be happy." Michelle handed Diana a fresh bottle to see if it would help.

The doorbell rang, and she went to greet the strangers. They introduced themselves as Mark and Anna. They looked to be a few years older than she was but seemed clean and healthy. Thoughts of a certain scene in the play *Annie* crept through her head, but she mentally chased it away. These people didn't want to adopt Grace for her money. She led the way to the kitchen.

Grace still fussed, but Anna went right to her, and took her from Diana's arms. She cooed and rocked as if there were nothing else in the world she'd rather do. Mark looked more unsure as if the cries weren't what he'd expected. Michelle repeated what she'd just told Diana and Kevin. Her parents had gone to meet Matt for the day. He was close enough they could make it without staying overnight, although it left Michelle alone to deal with this situation.

The couple stayed several hours, asking questions around Grace's screams. Anna offered to let Mark hold the baby, but he declined. Kevin exchanged a look with Diana, and she gave him a half-hearted smile.

"So, how often does she have these fits?" Mark asked.

"Not often. This is maybe the fourth time in a month."

Michelle hoped that seemed like a lot more than she made it out to be. "Usually, she's pretty easy."

"A month? And she's what—six weeks old now?"

"She'll be two months next week."

"Did the doctor say how long it takes for them to grow out of ... this?" Mark waved his hand in Grace's direction as if swatting away a pest.

"No. He just said we'd keep an eye on it and make sure it didn't get worse." Michelle tried to reign in her frustration. It's not like Grace wanted to be unhappy.

Mark nodded, but the frown lines didn't leave his forehead for the rest of their visit. Shortly after Mark and Anna left, Diana headed out too, mentioning that maybe she could bring them back on a better day. While Kevin stayed in the kitchen with Grace, Michelle picked up stray dishes from the living room.

"How much did Michelle pay you to cry the whole time?" Kevin asked the baby.

"I actually didn't."

"But, you're probably not unhappy about it." He raised an eyebrow.

"I can't say that I am." She pushed in the chairs around the table. "If he's going to be turned off from having her as a daughter because she has some bad days, then he doesn't need to be a dad, period. I know that sounds harsh, but what's he going to do when she's a teenager?"

"True point." Kevin laughed.

Michelle leaned against the counter and stared out the back window. Her mom's butterfly garden was blooming, and several of the insects fluttered around that corner of the yard, flitting from flower to flower. It was easy to imagine Grace playing out there when she was a little older, chasing the winged creatures.

"Kevin, what if I were married?"

"What?" He looked up from kissing Grace's cheeks.

"Is that the only reason you're not sure about me adopting Grace?"

"It's the main reason I can't even let myself think about it." Kevin shrugged. "I mean, if that weren't in the way, I'd have to look at other things too. Like your husband. But it would clear a hurdle. Why?"

"Just thinking."

"Michelle, please don't go do something stupid over this." Kevin moved the baby to his shoulder. "Marriage isn't something you can just jump into."

"Oh, wise bachelor, tell me more." She grinned to show she was teasing. "I know that. I'm not going to do anything stupid. But Greg and I have been talking. And I'm thinking about accepting his offer."

"The Greg you swore up and down was just a friend?"

"Yes. Friends are allowed to marry."

"I know that. John and Leah were friends before they got married." Kevin bounced and swayed as Grace's eyelids began to droop. "But they didn't just decide one day that they were supposed to get married. It was gradual."

"I love Greg. Always have." The fact that she loved him like a brother didn't need to come out right now. After all, even some Bible characters told little white lies to protect the innocent. And Grace fell into the innocent category. Right?

Kevin didn't look convinced.

"Greg and I have been friends since we were born. What's more gradual than a friendship that has lasted twenty-four years?" She splayed her hands on the counter.

"At least promise me you'll pray about it first. Michelle, even if Mark and Anna do decide they want to adopt Grace, nothing is final yet. Don't rush this."

Michelle drew an X over her heart. "I promise."

After he left, Michelle picked up her phone and called Greg. "We need to talk."

CHAPTER 15

When Michelle had asked to meet him at the local park, Greg's heart leaped with hope. But also twinged with dread. She hadn't told him how the visit with Grace's potential parents went earlier. Had it caused her to change her mind?

"Tell me how long you've thought about this." Michelle sat beside him on a bench that faced the pond. Grace dozed peacefully in the shade.

If he knew what to say, this scenario would be just about perfect. How was he supposed to admit to having loved her forever? Imagined her as his bride even when they were high school. Would she even believe him? Would it scare her away?

Several kids chunked bread pieces at the ducks, who dutifully dove for the morsels. Wind rippled the surface of the pond and blew back their hair. His thoughts scrambled over themselves faster than the waves spread across the water.

"Hello." Michelle waved her hand in front of his face. "Earth to Greg. Did you hear me?"

Maybe he could avoid saying too much by clarifying? "About us getting married?"

"Yes."

"I don't know." He blew out his breath in a huff. "I guess several times over the years."

Her gaze flew to his.

Oops. That might have been too much. "It's hard not to consider it every now and then when everyone around you expects it to happen." He leaned forward, elbows on his knees, wishing he could understand the expression on her face. "It occurred to me the other day that it would solve your problem. And it didn't strike me as a bad idea, so I decided to suggest it."

"So, it was completely based on logic?"

"Doesn't it sound logical?"

"No. Nothing about this sounds logical. It goes against everything in our relationship and changes it. How is that logical? What we've had all these years is a good thing. I guess I'm needing to know how much this is going to mess it up." She clasped and unclasped her hands in her lap. "I don't want to lose you as a friend."

"Mickey, husband and wife doesn't mean you can't be friends. I've had a lot of people tell me their friendship got better after they were married." One of his knees bounced in an erratic rhythm.

"But I don't like you in that way." She made a face like she'd eaten something sour. "It would be like marrying my brother."

"You said that the other night." And each time she repeated it, the knife turned a bit more in his chest. He took a deep breath, trying to ease the pain, and faced her more fully. "I know it wouldn't be the traditional sense of marriage. But in some ways, it would. Families used to set their children up to be married, and those people didn't even know each other. We're a step ahead of them."

Michelle shook her head. "What are our families going to say?"

"You don't think they'd be happy for us?"

"I think they'd see through our ruse and worry about us. At least our moms would."

"Already picking on your mother-in-law, and you haven't even accepted yet." Greg reached over and brushed back a strand of her hair. "It wouldn't be easy. I know that. But if we want it to work, we can make it work."

"What if one day we don't want to make it work?" Her shoulders slumped.

"If you go into it thinking things like that, then failure's more of a possibility. If you don't give yourself that option, it's not going to happen. Marriage isn't only about feelings and mushy stuff. It's about trust and respect and teamwork." He tilted his head to the side. "And love."

Uh oh. He said the *L-word.* Love.

"You said it wasn't just about feelings and mushy stuff."

"Real love, not the kind of love the culture talks about today. This isn't like or desire. Or even lust." He tapped his chest. "This is *agape* love—1 Corinthians 13 love. The kind of love that says, 'I want the best for her no matter what it means for me.'"

"You could really love me like that?" She studied him, obviously still unsure.

"I always have." And he always would. Whether she accepted his proposal or not. He squeezed her arm. "You're my best friend. How could I not want what's best for you?"

They sat in silence, the only sounds the children, the birds, and the lap of the water. How he longed to know what was running through her mind. Michelle looked down at Grace for a long moment. Her shoulders straightened, and she turned to face Greg fully.

"Okay."

"Okay?" He raised an eyebrow.

"Okay. I agree to this, but please, can we take things a little bit slow? I need to wrap my head around— I may need to work up to— to thinking of you as more than just a friend."

She agreed! He clasped the edge of the bench to keep from yanking her into his arms and shouting out his praise. It was a dream come true. Except for the look of uncertainty still lingering around the edges of her face. First Corinthians thirteen love. He needed to put her desires ahead of his.

"All right." He paused and then nodded. "I know it wasn't the kind of proposal that every girl dreams of. Maybe that's better in our case, but can I at least kiss your cheek?"

She let out a small laugh. "Yes."

He gently pressed his lips to her skin.

They agreed to tell their families tomorrow at Sunday lunch. That gave them not even twenty-four hours to wrap their minds around it. And brace themselves for whatever reaction their moms would have.

THE MARSHALLS HOSTED SUNDAY DINNER. Sheila laid out a scrumptious feast of baked chicken, creamy rice, and lemon-steamed broccoli, which she insisted made the meal healthy enough they could all indulge in the chocolate éclairs she'd whipped up for dessert. Sheila adored baking and enjoyed finding new recipes for days like today. As Michelle bit into the flaky dessert, she couldn't be more grateful.

As the conversation carried on around them, Michelle's mind wandered. She'd felt that slight caress of Greg's lips on her cheek the whole way home yesterday. He'd kissed her forehead over the years, sort of in a brotherly fashion, but this time was different. Was it because they were changing their relationship? Was it just an expectation?

Greg squeezed her shoulder as she popped the last bite in her mouth. She glanced his way, and he raised an eyebrow. The time had come to tell everyone their announcement. She licked the chocolate off her lips before giving him a little nod.

"I have—"

He started speaking just at the same time as Darcy did on the other side of the table. He motioned for her to go ahead with whatever she was about to say, but she shook her head.

After a moment of silent conversation between the siblings—a trait Matt and Michelle had never perfected, and she was always jealous of in Darcy and Greg—Greg conceded that he would go first.

"Michelle and I have been talking."

The table grew silent and still. Michelle refused to meet anyone's eyes but kept looking at Greg, waiting for him to finish the statement. He cut her a glance and a grin.

"We decided to get married."

"Oh!" Sheila exclaimed.

At the same time that Michelle's mom asked, "What?"

"Lisa, we've been hoping for this for years. That wasn't an excited thing to say." Sheila nudged her friend.

"It just took me by surprise, that's all." The look Mom gave her said there would be much discussion on this subject later when they were back home.

She glanced at Dad to see what he thought about it, but he just studied her. Was it that obvious that they were doing this for unusual reasons, or was she seeing the reactions she expected?

"Now, we'll be real sisters." Darcy got up and hugged her.

Michelle smiled.

"What about your announcement, Sis?" Greg asked.

Darcy shook her head *no* but then looked at Phillip and gave a slight nod. "It's not quite as happy as yours. It's, well, we're about to start a more intensive plan for fertility treatments. It's basically the last thing we can try. If this doesn't work ..."

"It will work." Greg emphasized his words by slapping the table with his palm.

"Think positive." Michelle wrapped her arm around Darcy and squeezed her again.

Grace started crying. Darcy stiffened and moved away from Michelle's embrace. Michelle wasn't sure what to do besides take Grace in the other room and change her diaper. Did her family suspect that she and Greg were getting married because of

Grace? She still couldn't believe it herself. And if she ended up keeping Grace but Darcy didn't get pregnant, what would that do to their family down the road?

~

THE DREAM TENDED to visit Michelle in the wee hours of the morning. This time, though, she wore a wedding dress. Her feet kept getting tangled in the multiple skirts and underskirts of the '80s-style, poufy dress, and she fought with the outfit to maintain control of her car's pedals. Her high heel snagged again, and she attempted to pull it free. She looked up just in time to see the headlights of Leah and John's truck right before it hit her car.

Once more, she fought her way out of the car after everything stopped spinning. She kicked off her ridiculous shoes and dashed across the street, not even caring that there was broken glass under her feet. She stumbled over to Leah and collapsed in a heap of satin and tulle. Leah reached out a bloody hand and grabbed the hem of Michelle's previously white wedding dress.

"Save Grace." Leah's voice was barely a croak.

"I'm trying to save Grace." Michelle ran a hand down Leah's arm. "I'm doing everything I can. I'm even getting married."

"No." Leah looked at her with a look of fierce protectiveness. "Save Grace."

Michelle awoke to find her feet twisted in her sheets. She worked to unwrap the covers from around her legs and shakily sat up. Wasn't she doing exactly what Leah had told her to do? She was attempting to save Grace, to keep her safe and loved and well. She got up and padded down the hallway to stand in Grace's door. The baby slept peacefully, completely unaware that anything was wrong.

May she always have such peace, God.

Michelle sat in the rocking chair and noticed the photo

album Diana brought the last time she was here. It was a collection she'd put together from the pictures they found in Leah and John's house. She thought Grace might want to have them as she grew up. Michelle flipped through the pages, trying to see what the real Leah was like, not just the dream-Leah.

Leah's long brown hair curled at the ends, and she shared Grace's big, blue eyes. Michelle could see why Kevin called Grace a 'Little Leah.' Kevin was in several of the pictures. John had been about the same height, with sandy hair. The love John had for Leah was evident when the camera caught him looking at her.

So much had happened in the last few days. At Jessica's wedding, she'd seen love like Leah and John displayed in these pictures. Darcy and Phillip were also a testament to love, despite the uphill battle they fought. Mom gave Michelle *the look* yesterday when Greg announced their engagement. Why? Because the love wasn't shining out of them like all these other couples? Would they ever have something like that?

"You okay?"

Mom stood in the doorway as if thinking of her had conjured her up.

"Did I wake you?"

"It's the curse of being a mother. Up with every little noise."

"Just dreaming again." Michelle wrapped her arms around her middle. "Leah is haunting me."

"You never even met her."

"No, but I feel like I have. Through the funeral, and Kevin, and Grace." She motioned to the crib. "She left a little piece of herself here."

"And that piece walks into your dreams?" Her mom looked skeptical.

"More like lies in the middle of the road, telling me to save her daughter."

Her mom shook her head. "You always did have a good imagination. Want to talk about it?"

"No. I'm okay. Just a lot on my mind."

"We will talk soon, though, right?" Mom asked. "I just get this feeling that some things weren't quite right about the announcement yesterday."

"I can't exactly go around not talking to you when we live in the same house." Michelle ducked her head.

"Your daddy taught you well."

Michelle looked at her questioningly.

"He always could answer a question without actually answering it."

Michelle grinned.

"Good night."

"Good night."

Why was she so afraid to tell her mom the real reason that she and Greg were getting married? There wasn't anything wrong with it. They were both mature adults who'd thought this through and knew what they were doing.

Engagement and marriage had always been vague possibilities in her future. Unlike most of her college friends who planned everything for their wedding except the groom, she didn't care what her dress looked like. Although, she'd rather not wear the '80s-style one from her dream. She absent-mindedly traced her left ring finger, and a little wave of disappointment rolled over her that Greg hadn't given her a diamond.

Sure, she'd told him not to make it too romantic since theirs wasn't that kind of a relationship, but it would have seemed more normal. And who knew? Maybe the romance would come with time? She gave a little nod. Besides, Grace was worth it.

CHAPTER 16

*H*e should have done this before now. Before he proposed. But there hadn't been time.

And then he'd put it off too long, half-expecting her to come to her senses and shatter the dream he'd been living for almost a week. Maybe that's why he'd been announcing it even knowing Michelle wouldn't be comfortable with it. The more people knew, the more it seemed likely to happen.

But now, he was going to make things right. Or at least as right as he could.

"If you'll write your budget down here, I'll pull some choices for you to look at and get an idea of what you might want." The clerk pushed a piece of paper and a stub of a pencil across the glass counter.

The light refracting off the jewels below him seemed to mock him as he wrote down a number that was hopefully high enough to get something decent. She deserved the best. But he was only a youth minister.

The clerk gave nothing away as he slid the pad back his way and then slowly unlocked the cases a little farther down and selected several different rings. "Do you know what your fiancée would like? Does she prefer round or princess or something else?

A newer trend is to go with another gemstone as the center jewel and diamonds as accents."

So many options. What if he chose wrong?

Focus, Greg.

"She's feminine but no-nonsense. A go-getter. A reporter and photographer." He'd imagined picking out a ring for her for years, but never to the point of actually picturing what to get.

The clerk nodded and moved to another section to grab something else. "Maybe something more like this?"

It was simple. Very basic. And nothing about it screamed *Michelle*.

"Not really."

"Okay." The clerk replaced the ring. "Do you know if she prefers silver or gold."

More decisions. Maybe he should have just brought her with him. No. He wanted this to be a surprise.

"Maybe this?" The clerk held out another choice. Silver. A square diamond sat in the middle, sparkles winking near the center.

Peace settled into Greg's stomach, and he nodded. "Yes. Perfect."

"Excellent, sir. Do you know her size?"

Greg closed his eyes and pictured Michelle's fingers. They were similar to Darcy's. Should he risk going with his sister's ring size? They could always get it refitted later if he was wrong.

Half an hour later, he walked out of the store, the weight of the ring pressing against his heart. There was no way he could keep this a secret long. Besides, they hadn't spoken since their argument. Time for a lunch date, if she could get away.

SEVERAL DAYS LATER, as Michelle sat in her cubicle, her phone rang.

"Ms. Wilson, this is Officer McLennon."

The policeman's voice on the other end of the line set her pulse racing.

"I wanted to let you know we caught him."

Michelle's heart stopped a second. She didn't have to worry as much when she drove at night because the man who'd caused her wreck was in custody.

"He'd made it all the way to Oregon. They're bringing him back here early next week, but nothing else will happen for probably a month. We'll let you know as things progress."

"Will I have to act as a witness or anything?" Her throat constricted at the thought.

"Since you didn't get a good look at him and we found him through traffic cameras, you won't need to testify. I just thought this might give you some closure."

"Yes." Michelle wiped her hands on her pants. "Thank you."

She ended the call and bowed her head. The peace she'd hoped would come didn't hang around long. Why was she so distraught about everything lately? She snapped at Greg yesterday when he'd announced their engagement to his youth group without asking her. Why had it upset her so much? Too many people were finding out about them too fast.

A couple of nights ago, she and Dad argued when she asked him how things were at the factory, and he accused her of working during off-hours. She and Mom walked on eggshells around each other. Even Grace must sense the tension because she'd been extra fussy the last few days.

Michelle's phone dinged. A text from Greg.

Want to meet for lunch?

Michelle mentally checked to make sure it wasn't one of his days to eat at school.

Where?

Diner?

Noon?

See you there

How many times had they had similar conversations? Shouldn't there be more to it now? But Greg kept it exactly as she'd requested. There were no added endearments. In a relationship like this, would they ever work up to a good-night kiss and an *I love you* at the end of the day? Was this worth it?

She glanced at the photograph of Grace pinned to her wall. That precious child had no one. Wasn't that enough of an incentive to give up the dream of a romantic marriage?

With an hour to finish up her "Dear Emma" article for this week, she read over the letter again.

Dear Emma,

How do you answer people when they ask you if you're pregnant yet? I'm twenty-two. My husband and I have been married for three years and aren't ready for kids. I try to be nice as I answer their nosy questions, but it's starting to bother me. Help?

No Baby-Bump Here

Why she'd picked this particular missive, she had no idea. She paused before typing. Could she ask Darcy what she told people? But then Darcy might figure out she was the one who wrote this article. She couldn't give away her anonymity. So far, she'd been able to keep the secret, and she only had a few weeks left.

Dear No Baby-Bump,

Be honest. Very kindly reply that you're not currently trying because you're enjoying it being just the two of you. You're still young. There's plenty of time to start a family. My chosen answer would probably be, "The moment I said, 'I do,' I considered us a family. We'll grow it later."

Hope that helps. Emma.

She hit *save* and closed the program before she changed her mind, then headed for her car. Would anyone ask Greg and her that kind of question? They'd already have Grace, but would people still ask when they'd start growing their family?

What would it be like to have a baby with Greg? The thought made her pause her steps across the parking lot. Would he or she have his blue eyes? Wavy hair? Dimples? She blinked a few times to try and get the mental picture out of her head. In this situation, a lot would have to change before a baby could happen.

Minutes later, she pulled into a parking spot and braced herself for the awkwardness.

Greg occupied the booth toward the back of the room, lounging in one of the same red leather seats where they'd spent many Saturday lunches as teenagers. Even the music playing from the jukebox in the corner was the same. She slid in across from him, and he looked up from reading.

"Hey." He set his phone aside.

"Hey, yourself. Is this a special occasion, or did you just not want to eat lunch alone?" She slipped her purse from her shoulder and leaned back.

"I thought when someone had a fiancée that he should eat with her at least occasionally."

"Hmm." If they weren't engaged, wouldn't they still eat together every now and then? They had before all this.

"I ordered for you." He stacked the menus back between the saltshaker and the napkin dispenser.

She raised an eyebrow and then changed it to a smile. No

need to get upset about it. He hadn't ordered for her because they were engaged. They'd known each other their whole lives. He knew she always ordered the chicken strip dinner. It wasn't like he'd take her out of her comfort zone. At least not when it came to food.

"You still mad at me?" He rested his elbows on the table, his hands clasped in front of him.

"No." She let out a breath. "You know I can't stay mad at you. I just wasn't sure I wanted it announced yet."

"Sorry, I didn't talk to you about it first. I didn't realize it would upset you so much." He folded his straw paper into a tiny little square and then unfolded it again.

"I didn't either. I guess I'm just on pins and needles about everything lately. The whole factory thing has me worried about Dad. Then, Darcy and Phillip have me feeling guilty because I have a child, and they don't. And Mom and I aren't speaking to one another because I get this feeling that she thinks what we're doing is wrong. You'd think she'd be happy."

"For one thing, your Dad is going to be okay no matter what happens to the factory. But worrying won't help. You've done what you can. You took amazing pictures for the article, spread out the reasons and thoughts about why things were happening in a way people will understand, and didn't try to offer up suggestions or plots that would only end in disaster—like what we did when we were kids."

"All my childhood plans were great." She threw her straw wrapper at him.

"Except that one for making money by offering to build ramps in friends' back yards for their skateboards. You got your Dad's old wood, some nails, and a hammer—and Stanley got a broken leg."

"One time." She held up her finger.

"Or the scheme to go door-to-door selling your homemade cookies, only you mixed up how much sugar and how much flour to use, so they sort of turned out a sickly-sweet runny mess, and you had to give everyone's money back."

"Finished?"

He studied her a moment as if to decide how mad she'd be if he brought up another failed project and shrugged.

"Okay, so my plans haven't always worked out the way I meant for them to. But that doesn't mean they weren't good."

"I like the one you're working on now."

"That's because it's yours." She pointed at him.

"But you're part of it." He caught her finger in his hands and pulled it down to the table.

"It just seems like there should be something that can boost sales at the factory enough to keep things going. I mean, surely there's some famous person out there who wants their own line of greeting cards or something."

Greg tilted his head. "Let me know if you find one, and I'll help you sweet talk them. Back to your worries: Darcy and Phillip will be okay. It's not easy for them to go through all this, but they'll come out of it still strong and in love. Don't let their struggles ruin your happiness. They wouldn't want that.

"Third, you need to talk to your mom. You're right. We're not doing anything wrong. I'll even talk to her with you if you want."

Michelle shook her head. "I'll talk to her soon."

Their food arrived, and she smiled. He'd even remembered to ask for extra gravy. They bowed their heads while he said a prayer. They'd automatically held hands during the blessing like they always did at family dinners, but this was the first time they'd done it alone. He gave her fingers a squeeze, and they dug into their dinners.

"What else is bothering you?" He reached across to steal one of her fries.

It never ceased to amaze her how much faster he ate than she did, even before her cast.

"They caught the guy who ran the red light." She took a sip of her tea. "The reason for our wreck."

Greg leaned forward. "Do they need you to come down and identify him or anything? Confirm he's the one?"

"I didn't even really see him." She shook her head. "Just the blur of the motorcycle as it raced through the intersection. I couldn't identify him even if I wanted to. They'll let me know as things progress."

"I'll go with you if you need to drive down."

"What if it's the week you guys go to camp?" She tapped open the calendar app on her phone and skimmed the coming weeks. "That's coming up in a month and a half."

"I'll work it out. I don't want you to go through that alone."

She nodded.

"I'm glad to see some things never change." She swatted at him as he stole another French fry.

"I'm still the same guy." He bent the fry in half and covered it in gravy. "Did you think I'd change just because we're engaged now?"

"Not really." She shrugged. "I don't know. This is nothing like I imagined my life."

"You never struck me as the type to sit and think about being engaged and getting married."

"Every girl thinks about it some. I mean, how can she not?" She ducked her head. "I didn't obsess about it like some girls, but there were certain things I expected that I won't get now."

"Like this?" He reached in his shirt pocket and pulled out a silver, princess-cut diamond ring.

"Greg!"

"You would have had when you agreed last Saturday, but the jeweler was closed by that time." He held it out on his palm.

She hesitated only a moment before reaching for it. If she took this, the situation would be more real. But the sparkle in his hand enticed her.

Just as she touched it, he snatched it away.

"What?" She jerked her gaze to his face.

"Gotcha." It was a stunt he'd been pulling since Kindergarten, holding up something she wanted and then taking it back at the last second.

"You going to make me jump up and down for it this time?"

"Nah." He held out his other hand.

She eased her fingers into his, the symbolism of giving him her hand not lost on her, and he slipped the ring on her finger. "You know my ring size?"

"I knew you were about the same size as Darcy and took a risk."

"It's gorgeous." She tilted her hand back and forth to admire how it caught the light.

"Does that help make it feel more real?" He nudged her foot with his under the table.

"It makes it feel more normal." She met his eyes as hers teared up a little.

He nodded. "You know, with that on your finger, you won't be able to keep it secret anymore."

"I know." She sighed.

"It's all going to work out." Greg took her hands.

She looked up into his familiar face, a face that was dear to her even if she wasn't romantically attracted to him. Maybe it would turn out like *Fiddler on the Roof*, and they'd grow to love each other. She smiled at him.

"Have you told Kevin?"

"Only that we were considering it. I was waiting to see if you'd back out—change your mind." She couldn't meet his gaze. In all the years they'd known each other, she'd never use the word fickle to describe Greg. He was dependable almost to a fault.

"Does that help convince you I won't change my mind?" He pointed to her ring.

She nodded.

"All right, then. Let me know what he says."

They paid their bill and walked out to her car. The diamond was even more dazzling in the sunlight.

She leaned back against her car and stared up at him, then crossed her arms to focus on the conversation instead of the new piece of jewelry. "What if Kevin still says, 'No'?"

"Why do you always borrow trouble?" He chucked her under her chin. "Don't you remember what the Bible says? 'Therefore, do not worry about tomorrow, for tomorrow will worry about its own things. Sufficient for the day is its own trouble.'"

"Well, since I was planning to call him today, that verse doesn't really work." She rolled her eyes.

"Let's pray about it, and then you can leave it in God's hands."

He took her hands in his once more, and they bowed their heads. With his mouth was close to her ear, she could hear him over the road noise. His breath stirred the hairs on that side of her face and made it hard to concentrate on the words he sent heavenward.

"God, we come to You today to thank You for our friendship. It has helped us through so much already in this lifetime, and we praise You for blessing us each with such a great best friend. Please be with us as we continue to make decisions about our life together, as we travel down a road we might not have considered before now. And, God, we now ask You to help us as we try to adopt Grace.

"Michelle feels like You brought Grace into our lives for a reason, and we're trying to live that out with our actions. Please bless Michelle as she talks with Kevin and give him an open mind to this idea. Help us all to make the best decision for Grace's life. Thank You for the time we had to spend together at lunch, and please be with us both as we go about the rest of our day. We love You and praise You. In Jesus' name, Amen."

Okay. Michelle took a deep breath. It was in God's hands now. All she had to do was wait on His will. Easier said than done.

"Guess we both better get back to work." Greg kissed her temple and then let her go.

Michelle slid into her car and watched him walk to his Jeep. His kiss lingered on her skin. When had his touch started doing that? What was wrong with her lately? She shook her head and started her car. One of the best features of this new vehicle was that she could plug her phone into the sound system and have hands-free talking. She dialed Kevin's number.

"Hey, Kevin, it's Michelle."

"You calling about the news?"

Did he already know? Had he guessed she and Greg would do this even before she knew?

"Michelle? Didn't Officer McClennon call you too?" Kevin's voice sounded worried.

"Oh." She mentally hit herself upside the head. Of course! "Yes. He did. Sorry, a lot on my mind. That's great news that they caught the guy."

"I thought so too." He paused. "Gives me a little more peace of mind."

"Yes."

"How's Grace?"

After a few moments of relating all Grace had learned in the last week, she got right to the heart of the matter. "Greg and I are engaged."

Kevin was silent on his end of the phone.

"I know you're going to tell me I'm crazy. But Greg and I talked it all through. He loves Grace, too, and we both want what's best for her. So, I agreed to his marriage proposal." She repositioned her left hand, so the ring caught the sunlight through the windshield.

"You've prayed about it?"

"Yes. And we're still praying about it. This is the way we feel God is leading us in our lives. And yes, one of the best parts is that maybe you'll consider me—us—now as possible parents for Grace."

"You do seem determined." Was that sarcasm in his voice?

"That's a good thing, right?"

"If you fight as hard for her the rest of your life as you have to keep her now, then yes, it's a good thing."

Michelle couldn't stop the grin spreading across her face. "What do we need to do next? Should we get married right away? Our moms were talking about a fall wedding, but we can move it up if we need to."

"Don't rush. We'll go ahead and start the paperwork and background checks—stuff like that. Figure out where you'll live, and we can do some home visits. But she's waited this long for new parents. I'd say she's still in good hands where she is."

"Thanks, Kevin." Emotion clogged up her throat again. "Thank you so much."

"Don't thank me yet. We've still got to see if you pass all the tests the state puts on you."

"How can we fail? Things are finally going right." She wiped a stray tear off her cheek.

"Keep praying about it, and I will too. I'll have Diana get started on that paperwork."

Michelle turned her phone off right when she reached the newspaper office and sat in the car for a few extra moments, debating whether she wanted to take her ring off before going in. Might as well face her fears sooner rather than later. What could people say besides *Congratulations*?

"Hey, Michelle, are you free tomorrow afternoon?" Hugh asked as she walked past his cubicle. "I need a photographer."

"What time?" She paused and leaned against his doorway. "I have an interview with the head librarian at ten to discuss the opening of the revamped children's wing."

"How about three?"

"Okay. What's it for? A story you're working on?"

"My story. Mine and Vanessa's. I'm asking her to marry me and thought she might like to have it on film." He leaned back in his chair with a grin. "I'll pay you, of course."

"Don't worry about that." She frowned. "Where are you doing it? Isn't that time a bit strange?"

"She's a kindergarten teacher, so I thought I'd surprise her at the end of the day."

"You might want to wait until all the kids are gone. Seems like they hung around forever when my mom was teaching." Michelle tapped her fingers against her chin. Too late, she noticed the direction of his eyes and realized she'd used her left hand.

"I see Greg beat me to the punch."

"How did you know it was Greg?" She folded her arms across her chest. "I told you the other day we're just friends."

"Every boy in town knew you'd someday end up with Greg Marshall. I told you the other day why all those so-called relationships in high school never lasted. They didn't want to stick around long enough to get their hearts broken. Every guy had a crush on you, and every guy knew you were unattainable."

"Every guy? You've got to be kidding." She scoffed. "I wasn't that popular."

"Every guy." He leaned forward. "Trust me. You weren't in the boys' locker room."

"A fact for which I'm still grateful, but I think you're exaggerating. There's no way every guy in the school wanted to date me." She straightened and pointed at him. "That would include you."

Even as she said it, she wanted to pull the words back in her mouth. His face told her she was right—he'd had a crush on her in high school. Her mind reeled from the implications as he turned back to his desk. She chewed on her bottom lip.

"So, want to leave here at three then? Will that give her enough time to pretty much have things cleared out?" Hugh shifted some papers around on his desk.

"Let's leave at three and pick up flowers on the way. That should give her enough time, assuming she doesn't book it home as soon as possible." What a day!

"She never leaves the school until at least four. But the flowers are a good idea." He gave her a quick nod before opening a new document on his computer screen. "Let's plan on that."

She started toward her cubicle but then paused. "I'm happy for you, Hugh."

"I'm happy for you too."

What was going on? Did she just make friends with Hugh Winters? Had he changed that much over the years, or had they both finally grown up? Or was she getting to know him as more than an opponent for class president?

She fully scratched his name off her stupid imaginary list. Then, mentally tore up the whole thing and threw it in an imaginary wastepaper basket, lit it on fire, and blew the ashes out to sea. With so much going on in her life, she didn't need a list like that.

Like a best friend whose kisses seemed to leave a mark on her skin. And a baby who might become hers in the near future. And a dozen articles to write before the end of the week.

So, if everything was finally starting to go right in her life, why did it still seem unsettled?

CHAPTER 17

"$\mathcal{I}$ know you don't want to talk to me, but I need you to tell me the whole story."

Mom cornered Michelle as she pulled a load of laundry out of the dryer while Grace napped.

Michelle continued her task until the laundry basket was full, then meticulously loaded the clothes from the washing machine into the dryer. She cleaned out the lint filter, tossed in a few wool balls for static control, and slowly turned the knob. When there was nothing else she could do, she picked up the basket with her good hand and faced her mother.

"Only if you help fold clothes."

Her mom straightened from where she leaned against the doorframe. "Of course."

They sat on either side of Michelle's bed with the laundry between them. There weren't that many clothes to fold, but Michelle needed something to say. She'd honestly wanted to look at Mom and say, 'Butt out,' yet another part of her was desperate for someone else to know the whole truth.

"Greg proposed to me at Jessica's wedding. Well, at the reception. He said he'd been thinking about it since Kevin said I couldn't adopt Grace because I'm not married."

Mom stopped folding and looked at Michelle.

"I told him 'No.'" Michelle tossed a onesie onto a pile. "I've never felt that way about him. He's just Greg. Whenever I considered who I might marry, it wasn't him."

Mom picked up a tiny pair of pants.

Michelle put down a shirt. "He made all these arguments about how it was a good idea because it would make me happy. And, I'd have Grace. So, I pointed out that I didn't love him in that way. He said it didn't matter. I said he could find someone down the road he actually did love in that way, and he might rather be with her. He said he wouldn't even look."

"And now you're engaged." Mom's voice had an edge to it.

"Not because of that night. That night, I was furious with him." She threw a pair of socks across the bed. "I thought he'd ruined our friendship. I told him I'd just make him miserable for the rest of our lives, and he said I should pray about it. I didn't plan to even think about it again."

"So, what happened?" Mom's confusion was evident in her voice.

"That couple came by to see Grace." Michelle ducked her head. "I could see the way the guy was looking at her when she cried, as if he wanted nothing to do with something so noisy. And I didn't want him to have the chance. Greg told me the offer still stood. I asked Kevin what he'd think if I were engaged. He told me not to do anything stupid."

"Do you feel like you're doing something stupid?" Mom leaned on one hand.

"Not as much anymore." She hugged a romper to her front. "When I first considered it, I thought I was going insane. But Greg and I got together and talked it all out on Saturday after that couple left. I made the same points again, and he countered them. And it just made sense."

"What made sense?"

"Getting married." Michelle shook her head. "Suddenly, it seemed like the right thing to do. So, I told him I would."

"But you kept the details out of your announcement on Sunday."

"It wasn't that we meant to cover anything up so much as we just didn't feel the need to elaborate." She shrugged. "I mean, Darcy and Phillip had their own announcement."

"But marriage isn't just some sort of mutual agreement. It needs to be more than that. If your marriage is built around having Grace as a daughter, what will you two do when she graduates and moves away? You'll be stuck for the rest of your lives, and she won't be there to hold you together."

"Well, we've already agreed that there's no getting out of it." Michelle picked up a pile of underwear and carried them to her dresser. "So, you don't have to worry about your daughter getting divorced or anything. If I'm miserable, I'll just stay miserable. Grace is worth it to me."

"Michelle Denise, do you hear what you're saying?" Mom stood. "You're already thinking that being miserable is a possibility. That's not the attitude someone newly engaged should have. Why is it so important to you to adopt Grace? I mean, I know you were in the same wreck, but other than that, you had nothing to do with these people. Why are you so desperate to do this?"

Michelle faced her mother. "Because it's my fault she's parentless."

She hadn't meant to say it. She'd been holding those words in for over a month. But she was tired of having them right on the tip of her tongue and not saying them. Mom's face transformed from frustration to despair. In two strides, her mother crossed the room and pulled Michelle to her.

"Oh, baby. It's not your fault Leah and John died that night. You did everything you could to stop it."

Tears streamed down Michelle's face as she leaned into her mother's embrace. How could she ever make her mother understand? She didn't even fully understand herself.

"If I hadn't stayed out so late, if I hadn't looked up at that stupid plane, if I'd paid more attention and swerved the other way—they'd still be alive."

"You don't know that." Her hair tickled Michelle's ear as she shook her head. "You didn't cause the wreck. That guy on the motorcycle did."

Michelle leaned back. "I forgot to tell you. They caught him."

"Him?"

"The guy on the motorcycle. He'd made it all the way to Oregon and should be in Little Rock tomorrow."

"Do you have to go down?" Mom brushed a tear from Michelle's cheek.

"Officer McLennon said he'd keep me updated as things progressed but that I probably wouldn't have to."

"We'll go with you if you do." Mom squeezed her arms.

"Greg already insisted on going."

Mom took a deep breath and studied her for a moment. "Michelle, please listen to me with an open heart. You know we love Greg like a son. And, yes, Sheila and I have dreamed of you two getting married. But I don't want you to get married just for Grace. You need a better reason than that."

"I don't need a better reason. And Greg agrees. It was his idea in the first place. I offered to let him out of it, and instead, he gave me this ring."

Mom grabbed Michelle's hand and studied the diamond.

"Please trust us." She squeezed her mother's fingers. "You and Mama Sheila raised us right. We'll be okay."

"I don't want you to end up unhappy."

"I'm marrying my best friend. He's made me happy my whole life. Don't you think he'll still do that after we're married?"

Michelle fed her mom practically the same reasons Greg had given her. If they worked for her, why didn't they work for her mom?

"I'll keep praying. I'm still uncomfortable with this, but we're here for you both. Just please keep thinking about it and praying.

Marriage isn't something to jump into lightly. I love your father deeply, but that doesn't mean our life together has been easy or that we've always liked each other through everything. Make sure Greg is truly the man you want to wake up next to every morning for the rest of your life before you take vows."

"I promise. But I really think we're doing the right thing."

Mom kissed Michelle's forehead and left her with the folded laundry. Emotions warred within Michelle as she leaned back against her headboard. Her mom was right, but Greg was right too. And she knew God had placed her in Grace's life for a reason. How could this not be the direction He wanted her to go?

"God, please, if this is what You want, can You give me some peace about it?"

HUGH EVIDENTLY THOUGHT of this as a secret mission instead of just a trip down a mostly empty school hallway so he could propose. Michelle followed behind him as he stayed close to the walls and peeked around corners before making each turn. She could almost hear theme music in her head and secretly started referring to this afternoon as *Mission Engaged*. He stopped at one last turn and waved her over to him.

"Vanessa's classroom is the third on the left. It has two doors. You take this door, and I'll go to the other. I'll sneak in and surprise her. You catch it on film. Got it?"

"Got it, Agent Eighty-six. And will this film self-destruct in ten seconds?" She playfully bumped his shoulder with hers.

He gave her a funny look, then caught her meaning and stood a little straighter as he worked at the knot in his tie. "Very funny."

"Go on. It's going to be fine." She nodded in the direction of the room.

"What if she says, 'No'?" He turned back at the last second.

Michelle blinked. "You'll never know until you ask her. Right?"

She followed him down the hall, then stopped at the far door and waited until he walked through his door before she cracked open hers. Vanessa's attention fixed completely on Hugh when he walked up to her with the flowers. Michelle snapped a few photos and watched through her lens as he got down on one knee.

Snap, snap.

Vanessa nodded and wiped away a tear.

Snap, snap.

He slid the ring on her finger.

Snap.

They hugged and kissed.

Snap.

Michelle snuck away without interrupting their moment, planning to edit these and give him a CD tomorrow. She ambled down the hallway alone now, winding her way through the familiar school. Had she ever imagined anything close to what her life was like now? Had she imagined anything past kindergarten? She shook her head.

Back at her car, a tear dripped from her cheek as she slid behind the wheel. Why was she crying? She wiped away the moisture with the back of her hand. Her ring scratched her cheek, and she examined the diamond again. Was she simply jealous that Vanessa had gotten the proposal Michelle wanted, something thought out beforehand, slightly romantic, by a man she loved?

She took a breath and started her car. If she didn't stop thinking, she'd go crazy. Or maybe crazier was the correct term.

When she got home, her first stop was to check on Grace, content in the playpen. "Hey baby girl, did you have a good day?"

No answer, but a beautiful smile.

Laptop open, Michelle pulled up the files for Jessica's wedding. Since Jessica planned to meet her this weekend to go over them and get her book and CD, Michelle needed to have them polished and to the printer tomorrow. So many sappy wedding poses.

Groom with groomsmen, trying to look cool. Bride with bridesmaids gushing over the bride's ring. Groom with bridesmaids. Bride with groomsmen. Bride and groom together. Bride and groom with wedding party. Bride and groom with family. Flower girls doing very unladylike poses right in the middle of the wedding.

She was happy with all the pictures except one.

"The lighting was right." Her fingers tapped a rhythm on her chin. "And the pose is okay."

Why did the moment they were announced as 'man and wife' bother her so much? Smiles on both faces. No craziness going on with the flower girl in the corner. No one moved between her and the stage. It was aesthetically perfect.

The photo was from the angle where she could see the groom's eyes looking into Jessica's. Pure love shone in that look. There was no other definition.

Once she saved everything to a CD, she uploaded the pictures to the website she ordered prints through. Then, she plugged her camera into the computer to upload the photos from today. It was like a stop-action movie. Every scene was accounted for. The lighting in the room had been perfect, with the afternoon sun angling through the windows, casting a glow on the couple.

She cropped and fixed contrast and sharpened edges. The next-to-last picture, where Hugh stood to hug Vanessa, made Michelle pause. Vanessa had always been gorgeous, but there was something extra in this picture. Vanessa was literally radiant, not just from the sunlight, but from happiness.

Michelle looked up and studied her own reflection. She and Vanessa were both newly engaged, so they should have the same glow, right? Instead, Michelle's face looked tired. Her shoulders slumped, and her eyes had no sparkle.

"Where are your toes?"

Sounds of Dad playing with Grace in the living room carried down the hallway. The little girl had found her laugh, and it rang out with clarity over and over again at his antics. It was the happiest she'd heard his voice in several weeks.

The cheerfulness lured Michelle from work and down the hall to catch a picture of it. "Hey, Dad."

"There's my reporter girl." He grinned up at her from the living room floor, where he sat tickling Grace.

"I thought you didn't want me to be a reporter at home." Much as she tried, a bit of bitterness crept into her voice.

Dad sighed. "I'm sorry I lost my temper with you the other day. Things are still so up in the air. The not-knowing is almost more stressful than the thought of the owner selling the factory."

"Any updates?" It was a risk to ask, but she couldn't resist.

"Most of the factory workers are back working. The protests only lasted a few days. I guess they figure they'd better earn a paycheck while they can."

"That's good, right?"

"But all of their jobs remain on the line. No decision has been made. The lawyers are still negotiating terms, but the two companies can't agree on everything. The current owner is fighting with all his might to keep the factory in town, but Southern Wishes keeps arguing the other location is closer to the interstate."

Michelle lowered herself to the floor beside him. Dad tried to leave his anxiety and stress at work, but it remained in the way he held himself, in his eyes. It amazed her how much they looked alike. Why did she appear so down when it was supposed to be a happy time? She had a solution for adopting Grace, she had her dream job, she was back in her hometown, and the bad guy had been caught. What more did she want?

CHAPTER 18

The rain left wobbly rivulets behind as it ran down the windowpane outside Michelle's cubicle. She needed to work on her "Dear Emma" column for the week but couldn't find inspiration to answer any of the letters in her stack. She also had an article due about the high school seniors' Project Graduation. This year they were adding a gazebo to the school grounds. She needed to get it done by this afternoon, but the shower mesmerized her.

"Those pictures turned out great." Hugh paused as he passed her cubicle. "Vanessa was excited when she saw them. She said she's going to use them to make it 'Facebook official.'"

"I'm glad I could help." Michelle mustered up a smile out of her dreary mood.

"Anything I can assist you with?"

She shook her head. "I just need to quit procrastinating."

Hugh leaned in closer and whispered, "Your Emma letters have been much better than the girl before you."

Michelle spun around, certain she'd hidden the letters whenever she wasn't working on them. "How did you know?"

"They sound like you. And you're the newest member of the

staff, so I figured Aunt Emma would assign it to you while Betsy was out with her baby. You just confirmed it, though."

"Nosy reporter," Michelle muttered under her breath.

He continued to his office space with a chuckle. She did need to start working seriously on her article.

Her phone interrupted her several paragraphs into typing. "Hello?"

"Ms. Wilson, Officer McLennon."

"Yes, sir. What can I help you with?" She hit *save* on the computer, unsure how long this would take.

"I just wanted to let you know that Charlie Malone is officially in custody. His attorney says he just wants to get it over with, and he's accepting a plea bargain." He paused. "He's looking at a minimum of twenty years right now for manslaughter."

"Thank you." She tapped a pencil against her memo pad.

"If you have any questions, please don't hesitate to call. But it looks like this case is about wrapped up on my end."

"I appreciate all you've done. I'm sure John and Leah's friends will also be glad to know."

She ran her pencil over the letters of the suspect's name, where she'd jotted them down in her little notebook. After another thank you, they hung up.

As she passed Hugh, he looked up with a curious expression but didn't ask anything. Emma sat behind her desk, studying several papers. Michelle rapped on the glass, and Emma waved her in.

"What can I do for you? I've been meaning to tell you what a blessing you've been to our newspaper." Emma waved at the figures spread on her desk. "I think sales might have gone up a bit lately."

"I'm glad to hear that. Thank you again for giving me the opportunity."

"Not a problem. Was there something you needed?" Emma looked up for the first time.

"Yes. I just got a call." Michelle picked at a pen stain on her finger. "Little Rock police caught the guy who ran the red light in my traffic accident several months ago."

"Do they need you there to identify him or anything?" Emma tapped a stack of papers into a slightly neater pile.

"I don't think so, but I wanted to give you a head's up, just in case. Officer McLennon said the guy would probably take a plea bargain."

Emma tutted and shook her head. "Criminals have it so easy nowadays, skipping out trial and having years taken off their sentence for 'good behavior.' Still, I'm glad for your sake that he's locked up now."

"Thanks, Emma." Michelle chewed her lip, unsure how to reply. "I'll let you know if I do need to take off."

"Fine, fine. We've made it before with a smaller staff. Just keep me updated on how long you'll be off, if needed, so I can make sure everything is covered. And go ahead and do a few extra Emma letters." She shuffled through several stacks before finding what she was looking for. "Some new ones came in today."

Michelle took the envelopes from the editor's hands.

"Oh!" Emma fluttered her hands to catch Michelle's attention before she left. "I meant to tell you, you've only got a few more weeks, and then Betsy said she'd take over again. I made sure she didn't have any of that postpartum depression before agreeing. I can't imagine that would make her advice very sound, can you?"

"No, ma'am." Michelle somehow kept from rolling her eyes. "Sleepless nights with a newborn don't help much, either."

Emma laughed. "Well, you seem to have mastered it, so maybe she will, too."

Back at her desk, Michelle called Greg. "He's behind bars."

"What time do we need to leave?" His no-nonsense voice never ceased to be a balm to her soul.

"I don't even need to go. He's taking a plea bargain." She

rearranged some things on her desk to make room for the new letters.

"How do you feel about that?" He had his minister voice on now. "Is that the closure you needed?"

"I'm not really sure. In some ways, yes." She wrinkled her nose. "Although, Emma said something about him getting off easy by doing it that way."

"He's still getting jail time, though, right?"

"Probably twenty years."

"Doesn't sound like getting off easy to me."

She didn't answer. Something about the situation kept her gut churning and unsettled.

"Maybe we could drive down there next Friday. Talk to the officer in person and see if that helps you find some more closure." Greg offered a solution that had been hovering in the back of her mind.

"Maybe."

"We'll get you through this."

"You're stubborn." She hoped he could hear the smile behind her words.

"And you're obstinate. What's your point?"

Michelle rolled her eyes even though he couldn't see her. That was an argument they'd had for years. She agreed they could talk about it later, after she'd had time to process.

"You don't sound very happy." His voice was muffled for a minute, like he'd put her on speaker and walked away.

"I guess this rainy weather is getting me down or something." She studied the downpour outside.

"Well, you obviously need a distraction." There was a staticky sound, and then his voice came through clearly again. "Why don't you come to the End-of-School get-together Sunday afternoon?"

"I don't know, Greg." What would she do at a party for a bunch of teenagers?

"If you're going to be a youth minister's wife, you need to practice, right?"

She let out a huff of air. A youth minister's wife. That part of the equation hadn't dawned on her before now. What was expected from a youth minister's wife?

"Was that a yes?"

"We'll see." She doodled swirly squiggles all over the corner of her notes.

"I'll ask your parents if they can keep Grace that afternoon." His self-assurance wasn't so comforting now. "See ya later, Mickey."

She shook her head as she hung up. Was it weird the way they ended their conversations? What else could she say? Theirs wasn't a normal relationship. A glance at the clock reminded her to get busy. She had a doctor's appointment this afternoon to get her cast off. At least one of her articles had to be finished before then.

GREG CAUGHT her after worship services that Sunday. "Wear something comfortable. I'll pick you up around one, and we can make sure things are set up before two when the kids arrive."

"Aren't you eating with us today?"

He shook his head. "Just gonna grab a sandwich and get a few things ready. Why? Will you miss me?"

"For an hour and a half?" She rolled her eyes and maneuvered her arm around Grace to see her watch. "I think I'll survive."

He grabbed her wrist. "No cast!"

"No cast." Her smile was completely genuine.

"That way, no one will get distracted from the size of that huge rock you put on her finger." Darcy playfully punched her brother's arm as she walked by.

Greg, being the mature man he was, stuck his tongue out at his sister.

"She seems in a good mood." Michelle studied Darcy as she greeted someone else farther up the aisle.

"She hides her hurt well." He gave half a shrug.

"Are things not going well?"

"They're not sure yet. I think they have a couple more weeks before they'll know if the process worked or not." He tickled Grace under her chin.

Michelle nodded. "What exactly are we doing this afternoon?"

"Oh, you'll see. You'll see." Greg waggled his eyebrows. He squeezed her arm and then walked off to his car.

"What was that all about?" Her mom asked.

"He won't tell me what he has planned for this afternoon. That makes me just a bit worried."

"How bad can it be? I mean, they've got to be done by the time evening Bible study starts."

"We are talking about the same guy, right?" Michelle laughed.

"You're the one who's marrying him." Her mom nudged her toward their vehicle.

TEENAGERS GATHERED in the fellowship hall that afternoon, along with several parents. Greg chatted with everyone, making his rounds while Michelle hung in the background.

"What's wrong?"

"Just didn't want to get in the way." Michelle shrugged.

"You're not in the way. Come on." He tugged her hand. "Stick with me and help greet people. They should almost all be here now."

Once he was sure everyone had arrived, he got the group's attention. It looked like about fifteen kids and seven adults, counting her and him.

"Okay. You guys all talked me into it. I want you to divide

into five groups, so about three kids per group. At least one adult has to go with you."

The kids spent several moments shuffling around, trying to get in groups with their best buddies. When they were all organized, Greg handed out envelopes.

"Inside each envelope is a list of twenty items. Your team needs to go around with a camera—the one on your phone is fine—and collect pictures of all twenty things. First team back with all twenty pictures wins, but I'm not telling what the prize is yet. Do not open the envelope until you're in your car. Questions?"

There were several laughs as a couple of the groups quickly closed their envelopes back, but no questions.

Greg nodded. "Go!"

A mad scramble ensued. It was almost eerie how quiet things were after the high schoolers left. Michelle helped Greg prepare the snacks while they waited for the teens to return. She looked up and caught him staring at her.

"What?" She patted her hair to make sure it was still tamed.

He tilted his head to the side as he continued to study her. "You just look unhappy."

"Wow. Thanks so much." She finished pouring a bag of popcorn into a bowl.

"Hey. You know what I mean." He took a few steps toward her and pulled her into a hug.

"What if the kids come back?" Her words were muffled in his shirt.

"They know we're engaged. A hug won't be a bad thing for them to see."

She leaned her head against him. His heart beat steadily under her ear. Just like him.

"Worried about Friday?"

"I'm hoping it will get these stupid dreams to go away." She started to pull away, but he held on.

"You're still having the dreams?"

163

"Mostly the same." She rested her forehead on his chest. "Leah and John and the wreck. Right around the time we got engaged, I was wearing a really awful wedding dress in one."

He laughed and brushed her hair back. "An awful wedding dress, huh? I imagine you'd look good in any wedding dress."

"I don't know. This was a really poufy '80s-style gown. I don't think anyone would look good in it." She shook her head with a giggle. He thought she'd look good in any dress? Now, that was something a bride liked to hear.

The doors opened behind them, and they stepped apart.

"We need one more picture," Kyle, one of the juniors, said. He rushed up to them, his phone in front of him.

"Which one do you still need?" Greg leaned over to look at their list.

"A picture of a godly couple showing their love for each other with a kiss," Daphne read.

"Who came up with this list?" Michelle's words tangled with Greg's, who asked, "Why didn't you go to your parents?"

"There's a godly couple right here."

The kids looked pointedly at Greg and Michelle.

Michelle raised her eyebrows. Seriously? Talk about being put on the spot!

"When they have a point, they have a point." Greg's voice was soft in her ear.

"Greg, I'm not sure this is a good idea." Michelle's whisper was a bit frantic. "Maybe we should tell them we're one of those couples waiting for our wedding day to kiss."

"Are we?" His eyes seemed to investigate the depths of her, intensely locked on hers.

Another group noisily entered the room.

"Hurry. They might beat us!"

The first group jumped up and down, their cameras at the ready.

Michelle's heart pounded in her ears. Heat rushed up her

face as the embarrassment of this situation sank in. Surely, he would just kiss her cheek or forehead like always, right?

Time slowed down as he gently clasped her chin in his hand and tilted her head up. He leaned in, hovering for just a second before closing the slight gap between them. For only the briefest of moments, his lips pressed against hers, but she could still feel them when he pulled away. Had her heart moved to her ears? The pounding was deafening.

Then, everything sped back up to normal speed, as if someone had dumped reality from a bucket over their heads.

"Woohoo! We win!"

The first team did a victory dance.

Greg studied her as if figuring out if it had been okay. A little too late now. She jerked away and wove through the returning groups of teens and out into the hallway. What was wrong with her? The kiss hadn't been bad. It had been very sweet. But it still seemed so wrong, like her brother kissing her instead of her fiancé.

How would she ever be his wife if she couldn't even handle a simple caress like that? She rubbed her hands over her face and strode down to the empty auditorium.

STUPID.

He had to be the dumbest man in the whole world.

Why had he even added such an idiotic task to that list of pictures to take?

And now he couldn't even go and try to fix the situation because he was the one in charge of making sure everyone here was occupied. Absentmindedly, he helped dish out the snacks and fill cups. Once all were eating and chatting, he could slip away and hopefully find peace with his fiancée. Assuming she still wanted to be engaged.

"Isn't the picture great, GM?" Daphne held up her phone, the evidence against him shining from her screen.

If this were an ordinary romance, he'd treasure a photo like that. But nothing about this situation was normal. And somewhere in the middle of holding her earlier and seeing her wear his ring, he'd forgotten.

She wanted to move slowly, for things to stay mostly the same. And he'd flat-out kissed her. On the lips. In front of a bunch of teenagers.

Even in a normal engagement, that was probably wrong.

"Aren't you eating, Mr. Marshall?" Trevor came through the line for seconds.

"Not right now, Trevor. But you enjoy." He tossed a few more cookies on the growing boy's plate.

"I need to step out for a moment. Can you get the singing started in about ten minutes if I'm not back by then?" Greg caught Michael, one of the youth deacons.

"Sure, Greg. No problem." Michael glanced toward the door. "Relationships are hard enough without a bunch of teenagers around, huh?"

"Yeah." Greg offered a weak chuckle before he let himself slip away to find Michelle. Assuming she was still in the building.

There she was. About halfway up the auditorium, in her family's regular pew, staring up at the stained-glass window. Greg slid in beside her.

"I'm sorry." He let out a sigh.

"Me too."

"I had no idea they would choose us to be an example. The task was to find a godly example of everything on their list. And while I'm happy they think of us that way, I didn't realize it would bother you that much. Am I that bad of a kisser?" He nudged her a little with his shoulder.

"It wasn't that."

Evidently, she wasn't ready to give in to his attempt to lighten the mood.

"It's just like I told you when we agreed to all of this. I'm not ready for the romantic stuff yet. I haven't trained my brain to think of you that way. And I definitely didn't expect our first kiss to be witnessed by a bunch of teenagers. I mean, honestly, Greg. What were you thinking?"

"You're right." He nodded. "I should have told them no."

She hung her head. "I'm already shaping up to be a bad wife, aren't I?"

"Nah." He wrapped his arm around her shoulders like he'd so many times before. "We just both have a lot of work to do to make this work. Are we still on for dinner Tuesday night?"

"Of course."

Two days for this to simmer between them.

"Okay. I better go wrap things up before people start arriving for evening services. Save me a seat?"

She nodded.

With great effort, he moved away from her once more. In his dreams, he'd imagined their first kiss to be perfect. For her to want more, even. This, though. Was this something they could get past?

CHAPTER 19

"Mickey?" Greg's voice brought her back to the present. They sat in their booth on Tuesday evening, a few remains of their dinner on the table between them.

"Mm?" She shredded the piece of decorative lettuce.

"You're like a million miles away right now. What's going on?"

Michelle ate another French fry while trying to figure out what to tell him. Did he need to know what she'd admitted to her mother the other night? He was still her best friend. She shouldn't have kept it from him this long.

"Did you see the Little Rock paper this morning? There was an article about Charlie Malone—with a picture. His face ..."

Greg waited for her to go on.

She ran a hand over her eyes. "It killed me to see his face because it looked so much like the same one I've been staring at in the mirror for the last month and a half. The guilt behind his eyes, it's the same guilt that's been eating at me."

"Guilt?" He pulled her fingers down and wove them through his. "Why?"

"Because I blame myself for that wreck." She stopped his protest with a look. "I know what you're going to say, but there's

169

still this niggle in the back of my mind, saying, 'If only I'd left the party earlier, if only I'd swerved the other way, if only I knew CPR ...'"

"If you had swerved the other direction, you might have hit the tail of the motorcycle. And the way John was driving, I think his truck still would have flipped. And Leah still would have flown through the window because she wasn't wearing her seatbelt."

"I know all that in my head." Her chin dropped to her chest. "But there's still a little part of me that wants to argue."

"No, there's a little bit of Satan that wants you to have guilt and doubt. Because it helps him pull you away from God. For every seed of doubt and guilt that remains, be it earned or not, that's one little spot you're not letting God have in your life."

She let that digest a moment. There was no denying he made sense, but still ...

"It's why it's so important to me to adopt Grace. Because I'm the one who killed her parents. I have to make it up to her."

Greg nodded. "I think I'm finally starting to understand. Why didn't you tell me all this? I could have told you it wasn't your fault."

"I wouldn't have believed you." She cringed at the way that sounded. "No offense. I didn't believe my parents when they told me the same thing."

"This is me. Not your parents." He gently turned her head to face him. "You've always come to me with problems."

"I'd never done anything before that I felt so guilty about. I mean, I'm glad to know that you'll be there for me if I ever need to murder someone, but this is the first time someone actually died at my hands." She wrinkled her nose to show she wasn't serious.

"We'll just have to make sure the elders don't find out." He rolled his eyes. "But seriously, it was just a series of bad events that started when Charlie ran that red light. It didn't help that John was distracted, Leah had unbuckled, and you were tired.

But even if all those things weren't true, something else might have caused the same thing to happen. We'll never know. All we know is what did happen, and we have to live with it."

Michelle nodded.

"So, do you feel less guilty now?"

"After reading the article, I can see the wreck clearer." She picked at a spot on her pants where some gravy had landed. "My mind had warped it over the last few weeks, in my dreams and memories, to where all I could see was my part in it. Seeing the play-by-play written down—I think it did help. I'm not sure I'll ever completely get over it."

"Still feel like you need to adopt Grace?"

"You trying to get out of it?" She cautioned a glance his way. Why had her heart dipped at that question? Had she finally gotten used to thinking of them as engaged? Or was it something else?

"No. Just wanting to make sure you still needed me."

"I'll always need you, Greg." She squeezed his bicep. "You're my best friend. I'm sorry I haven't acted like it lately."

"You've been under a lot of stress." He tucked a stray hair back behind her ear.

"I just keep remembering that look on Charlie's face in his mug shot." Michelle wadded up her trash. "He looked like he'd never be able to forgive himself. I don't want him to feel that way. I know how it feels. I wish I could help him see that he can move past this."

"There's only One who can give him that ability." Greg piled their trash onto the tray.

Michelle nodded. "Do you think he knows Him?"

"We could introduce them."

Could they really? "Even though he's in jail?"

"Why not? Let me make some calls and see if he'd accept a visit. I have a friend down there whose church has a jail ministry. I bet he can help us figure it out. I told you we could drive down there Friday. The offer still stands. But maybe we need to talk to Charlie instead of the officer."

She nodded, and Greg led her out of the restaurant.

~

MICHELLE HAD VERY SUCCESSFULLY AVOIDED BEING in a jail. Until now. The threat of being locked away behind bars had always made her want to be good. Even though she wouldn't be here long, she couldn't shake off all of the willies as she and Greg followed the police officer to the room where they would talk to Charlie Malone.

He sat on the other side of the glass, his eyes wary and unsure. How old was he? Maybe early twenties. His face looked too young to hold that much pain. She and Greg shared the plastic chair on their side, and Greg held the phone between their heads so they could both hear. Charlie lifted his own set to his ear.

"Hi, Charlie. My name is Greg Marshall. This is Michelle Wilson."

Charlie glared at Michelle. "You here to see me in jail? I know it's where I belong."

"No." She shook her head. "No. I'm here because I wanted to tell you it wasn't all your fault. Every one of us in that accident played our own part, me included. And I wanted to let you know that—that you don't have to hang on to the guilt."

"Look, Lady. I know what the cameras caught. My attorney made sure I knew all the evidence they had against me. It was my fault. I decided to run a red light, and now I'm in jail." He paused, took a breath. "I killed two people."

"She's not saying it's not your fault that you ran the red light." Greg's voice remained calm. "She's just saying that everyone else made bad choices that night too."

"I've been blaming myself for the last six weeks." Michelle touched her chest.

"And now that you've seen me, you can quit blaming yourself." Charlie narrowed his eyes.

"No. Now that I've met you, I can see the big picture." She pointed between the two of them. "I played my part in the wreck. You did too. But Leah and John did too. If they hadn't been going quite so fast, if she hadn't unbuckled, they might still be alive."

Charlie shook his head.

"Look, I know you probably won't believe me right now, but please think about it. This has been a huge struggle for me. But I have someone to help me, besides my friends and family. I have a relationship with God. I haven't always worked hard enough to keep that relationship strong, but I can feel His hand in this. And I want you to know I'm praying for you to find some peace — peace can only come through finding Him."

Charlie's black hair almost hid his face as he hung his head, a tear trickling down his cheek.

"This is Grace." Michelle pulled a picture from her purse and slid it through the tiny slot in the window. "She's the blessing that happened that night. Even though Leah and John both died, their baby girl survived. She's what keeps me going in the mornings. God's hand is in this, and I pray it will be on you, too, Charlie."

His fingers traced the baby's face in the photo, but then he hung up his phone and slipped the picture in his pocket. Greg replaced their handset too, and the guard escorted them back down the hallway.

She swallowed several times before she could talk around the lump in her throat. "Do you think that did any good?"

"We may never know. But maybe it at least planted a seed. We just have to give God time to water it." Greg pulled Michelle close to his side as they came out of the building.

Kevin was about to enter as they stepped into the sunlight. They all stopped on the steps.

"What are you guys doing here?" Kevin pointed at the jail.

"We came to visit Charlie." Greg motioned behind them.

"I wanted to share with him a little bit of the peace I've found in this situation." Michelle hugged her arms around her middle. "And to let him know that I'm praying for God to give him some relief from his guilt."

"I was sort of coming to do the same thing." Kevin stared up at the brickwork above them. "I thought when I saw him, I'd feel nothing but hate and anger. And then I saw his expression in that newspaper picture. It just shot me through. No one deserves to hurt that much."

They all nodded.

"I'll try to come down here when I can and meet with him. Maybe he'll let me do a Bible study." Kevin shrugged. "I think it's what John would want."

"Let me know if I can help, man." Greg offered his hand before they parted ways.

It was a quiet ride home. Michelle had more peace about the wreck, but she still didn't have much about her situation with Greg. That would have to be worked out later. She was too exhausted to think about it now.

CHAPTER 20

"Did you see the paper this morning?" Dad asked Mom as Michelle entered the kitchen on Sunday.

"Um." Mom's eyes were fixed on her.

Michelle looked from parent to parent, waiting for one of them to tell her what was going on. Finally, she marched over and grabbed the newspaper out of Dad's hands. He stood up as if waiting for whatever reaction she was about to have. She unfolded it and shook it out so she could see the front page. There, right in front of her in full color, was a picture of her next to the mugshot of Charlie.

Local Journalist Finds Peace with Reckless Driver in Jail

She skimmed to the byline and saw Hugh's name. She willed her hands not to shake as she spread the paper on the counter to read the article.

Hugh hadn't made Charlie out to be a bad person, per se, but he also hadn't left any doubt of how he figured Michelle felt—and he figured wrong. Yes, she'd found peace, but not in the way

Hugh described. Not because Charlie was in jail. Peace had come when she finally realized the truth.

Hugh hadn't even asked her if this would be okay. Wasn't that her right as a citizen, not to mention a member of the newspaper staff? How could Emma approve this?

"Michelle, say something." Dad laid a hand on her shoulder.

"What can I say?" Michelle slowly ripped the paper in half. "I want a retraction."

As she finished getting herself and Grace ready for church services, Michelle tried to regain some control. In the backseat of her parents' car on the way to the church building, she willed herself to breathe deeply and evenly. She whispered a little prayer for restraint before they got out and walked in.

There he was. Halfway up the auditorium, Hugh chatted up several people with his fiancée. No. Despite the deep breaths and prayers, Michelle couldn't stop herself. She stormed over to where he stood, drew her fist back, aiming straight for his arrogant jaw.

But Greg's arms wrapped around her, restraining her before she could swing. Hugh held up his hands, his eyes wide with shock.

"How dare you!" Her voice came out almost shrewish. "You didn't find out details or get facts. You wrote that article on pure speculation. And you didn't even ask if I was okay with something like that being published. I thought we'd learned to trust each other and get along, but you've thrown away any chance of that forever."

Everyone around them backed away a bit, completely silent.

"How dare you?" Michelle strained against Greg's hold another moment, but he was stronger, and deep down, she knew she needed to give in and get away from the situation. She relinquished to his tugs and stepped away from Hugh. The traitor.

Greg pulled her away and dragged her down the hall and into his office. "Where's Grace?"

"With my mom." The words came out between sobs.

He sat her down on a bench and knelt before her. "Did you really think that was going to make it better?"

Michelle shook her head.

"Well, they won't think about that article now. They'll think about your insane outburst and your attempt to murder one of their beloved newspaper journalists. No offense, Michelle, but that was probably the stupidest thing I've ever seen you do." Greg stood and paced the small space.

She clenched her jaw and swallowed hard. Had he just said that to her? Wasn't her best friend supposed to back her up in everything? What had happened to him helping her hide the body if she needed to commit a murder?

"What do you want me to say?" She practically spit the words at him. "I suppose you think me walking out there and apologizing would help? It wouldn't be honest. I wanted to hit him, and I'm sort of mad at you for stopping me."

"You won't be tomorrow."

"Maybe not. But it's still today." She beat her fist against the wooden seat.

"And, of course, it looks even worse because you're the youth minister's fiancée." He leaned against a bookcase and folded his arms across his chest. "Seriously, Michelle. I don't understand you anymore."

Oh. Of course! He was mad because she made him look bad. Who cared that she was torn up inside by a whirlwind of righteous indignation?

"Well, that makes two of us." Her finger shook as she pointed it at him. "Because I don't understand you anymore, either."

Dad cleared his throat in the doorway. "Don't suppose I could talk with her alone for a bit, could I?"

Greg studied Michelle for a full minute, his jaw tightening and relaxing before he finally nodded and stepped out the door. Dad sat down beside Michelle and wrapped his arm around her, pulling her into his side. She leaned her head against his shoulder and let the tears fall freely.

"I'm sorry, Mickey. I should have made you talk it out with me before we came. I thought you'd gotten it out in that outburst at home. I should have known better. You always have been my fight-first-and-talk-later girl."

They stayed there through Sunday School. She was in no mood to face Hugh again any time soon, not to mention everyone who'd witnessed her outburst. But she also knew that until she calmed down and forgave Hugh, her heart wasn't in the right place for worship, either.

"I don't know how to fix it." Her voice came out in a hoarse whisper.

Dad sighed. "How about an apology to Hugh?"

"I'm not sure I can right now. I'm still so angry." She fisted her skirt in her hand and then released it, studying the wrinkles it left behind.

"How about an apology to Greg?" He nudged her shoulder with his. "Could you start with that?"

Michelle wiped her eyes and blew her nose. "I can at least try, right?"

"It's time to go in for worship."

"I'll be there in a minute. Let me go splash some water on my face."

He nodded and left her there. She slipped into the little bathroom off the secretary's office. The mirror showed her what she'd already feared—her cheeks were splotchy, and her makeup was pretty much gone. She splashed cold water on her skin until it at least looked somewhat better. With a deep breath, she left her sanctuary and headed to the auditorium.

She didn't make her way to where her parents sat, even though she knew her mom would be looking for her to come in. Grace's little head rested against her mother's shoulder in sleep, and her mother had proven time and again that she was a better parent, anyway. Instead, she slid into the last row and kept her head down for much of the service. She did try to listen, but not much sank in.

Part of her still wished she'd left a huge bruise on Hugh's face. The other part of her just wanted to understand why he'd written that article. Had Emma assigned it to him? Had he done it on his own after overhearing her phone conversations on the other side of the cubicle wall? She needed more privacy. How would she ever face her coworkers the next morning?

"Ride with me to lunch?"

Greg caught her hand as she started to slip out the door.

She opened her mouth to turn him down but then nodded. A quick wave to her mother gained approval of the plan. He handed her his car keys so she could wait outside instead of having to face anyone else. She scurried to his Jeep, slid in the passenger seat, and kept her head down. A tap on the window alerted her to Greg's arrival, and she unlocked the doors so he could get in.

"AFRAID SOMEONE MIGHT COME out and mug you?" Greg threw his blazer into the back with more force than necessary. At this point, he was as angry at himself as he had been at Michelle. As badly as she'd handled the situation, he hadn't made it better—except by keeping her from actually hitting Hugh.

"No. Just a habit from living in the city." She shrugged. "Lock your doors as soon as you get in."

"I'm sorry I said that about it being worse since you're the youth minister's fiancée." Greg glanced at her as he drove to Darcy's house. "I worked hard to live up to expectations. I mean, we grew up here, so I had to prove to everyone I wasn't the kid they'd known all their lives. In some ways, it's a blessing and a curse to be a youth minister at the same congregation where I was in the youth group.

"You understand that. You're sort of doing the same thing

with the paper. But that was still no excuse for me to say it to you. You didn't need more guilt than what you probably already felt."

Michelle stared out the window. "I didn't mean it when I said I wished you'd let me hit him. I told myself I was okay and wouldn't do anything stupid when I saw him, but then he was the first person I locked eyes on. Even though I was convinced I'd calmed down, I really hadn't. I'm sure everyone thinks I'm nuts now."

"No. But there's a lot of people worried about you. Several people asked about you as they left today."

"I feel so stupid." She let her head bang lightly against the window.

"Everyone makes mistakes now and then." Greg put his hand over hers and squeezed.

"But not like that. That was a big one. I just kept thinking about how Charlie would feel if he read that piece of garbage. I mean, I hope we made some headway with him, and that Kevin will continue making progress at reaching him. But if he saw the article and thought I felt that way—it would undo everything we said." She flopped her hand under his as if she'd forgotten his was there.

"Maybe you should explain that to Hugh tomorrow."

She let out a breath. "It won't be easy."

"The right things hardly ever are."

He parked in front of his sister's house but didn't move. She wore a look of dread on her face. Surely facing her coworkers wouldn't be that awful, would it? What else could she be so afraid of?

"You going to be okay?"

She swallowed and nodded. "Guess they're probably waiting on us, huh?"

~

DARCY AND PHILLIP'S house fit Darcy's personality to a *T*. Each room had its own color scheme and might have come straight off the pages of a magazine. It was comfortable in its own style but not how Michelle hoped to decorate her own home someday. She'd been here several times, and each time it looked a little more complete. Maybe now, though, Darcy had finally decided it was finished. Not much had changed since the last time Michelle had come over.

Those last few words Greg spoke in the car struck a chord with her, and she began to get a bad feeling about what she'd have to do in the near future. Could she face such a decision? Her actions earlier showed a lack of maturity. And definitely not enough strength. And strength was something she needed right now.

Michelle pitched in as much as she could in getting things on the table, but everything was pretty much done. Greg sat next to her in what had always been his designated place. They all bowed heads as Phillip said the prayer and then dug into the potatoes, green beans, and roast Darcy had prepared.

No one mentioned what had happened at church that morning. Was that why she was so uncomfortable, or was she simply still fighting her guilt? She'd have to come up with a way to apologize to Hugh soon. Just swallow her embarrassment and do it. She forked a piece of meat harder than necessary.

Darcy interrupted her thoughts by announcing that she and Phillip had news, then looked at her husband as if to decide who should tell it. He squeezed her hand, and she nodded.

"We got our test results back from this infertility treatment." She visibly swallowed. Everyone waited in silence for the good news that should come. "It didn't work."

A collective sigh went around the room. Sadness seemed to have personified itself and joined them at the table. Phillip wrapped his arm around Darcy's shoulders as she wiped a tear away.

"We've decided to quit trying to get pregnant." Her voice

wavered toward the end, but she didn't cry like Michelle imagined she would have.

"No!" Sheila said. Peter put his hand on her shoulders before she could stand up.

"It's not just a financial reason." Phillip flipped his knife over. "Although that is a huge factor. We've gone through this for a couple of years now, and the doctors have helped us through every option we have. We could continue putting ourselves through this month after month, forking out thousands of dollars, and stressing, and worrying, and dying a little bit each time it doesn't work.

"Or we can take that money and put it toward something that we know will end up with us having a child. We decided to go the second route."

"We're applying to adopt." Darcy put her hand over Phillip's to still its restless movement. "I guess both of your first grandkids will come that way."

A light bulb flipped on in Michelle's head. This was why she'd been in that accident, why she'd fought so hard to keep Grace. God had someone in mind to be Grace's parents, but it wasn't her and Greg. Her heart beat a little faster as understanding sank in, and she realized what the hard thing she needed to do was.

Her heart argued with all its might. The little girl sleeping quietly in the travel crib in the corner was a huge part of her life. How could she bear to give up that precious gift?

How could she not? Everyone was right—she wasn't ready for this. She wasn't responsible for the wreck and didn't have to carry the weight all on her shoulders. And she wasn't even ready for marriage, either, come to think of it.

No. This needed to happen, and she must start things working in the right direction before she lost courage. *Now.*

Michelle cleared her throat, but no one seemed to hear, so she stood up and waited until everyone was quiet.

This was it. Her heart pounded in her ears. "I want you guys to adopt Grace."

Everyone froze.

"I think it's what God had planned all the time." Michelle nodded her head as if to emphasize she knew what she was saying and agreed with it. "I just didn't see it until now."

"But Michelle—" Darcy started.

"No. I'm not ready to be a parent. I've proven that over and over again the last few months. Especially this morning. I'm not ready to put someone else's needs before my own. In fact, I'm not ready to get married. Greg, the only reason we decided to get engaged was to adopt Grace. I'm not holding you to that."

She slipped off her ring and set it on the table beside his plate. "Mom was right. It was the wrong reason to get married. I just didn't want to admit it."

Greg's eyes were wide, his mouth open, and he stared up at her. He shook his head almost imperceptibly. No one else seemed able to move or say anything. Michelle didn't want to sit back down and finish her last few bites of potato. She needed time to herself, to let everything sink in.

"I'll call Kevin and let him know what's going on. I'm sure he'll approve of you guys." She picked up her plate and carried it into the kitchen.

Darcy caught her before she could get to the front door. "Michelle."

She turned.

"Phillip and I would love to adopt Grace, but don't rush into this. You've fought for her for so long. How can you just let go of her now?"

Michelle squeezed Darcy's arm. "I love Grace. But I'm not what's best for her. It's time to pass her on to someone who needs her as much as she needs them."

Darcy hugged Michelle. "What about my brother? You crushed him back there."

"Greg?" She shook her head. "He'll be okay, even better now. He won't be stuck with me as anything more than a friend, and that's much better. The way it should be."

"Why don't you talk to him? This meant more to him than you realize. Don't leave it like this."

"I can't right now." She took a step back. "I need to go, sort things out, get it straight in my head."

"You're walking home?"

"It's only a few blocks, and I'm wearing flats. It'll be fine. Thanks for lunch."

She slipped out the door before Darcy could delay her any longer. Why had Darcy said she'd crushed Greg? He was just in shock that he'd gotten out of their agreement so easily. There couldn't be anything else. They were back to the way it should be, just Michelle and Greg. No crazy romantic things to get in the way or be confusing. Right?

WHAT HAD JUST HAPPENED? Greg dodged his sister's hands as she reached for him. He couldn't talk right now. Couldn't be around people anymore.

One minute, they'd been engaged, his dream come true. He'd even suspected Michelle was warming to the thought. Then, today everything had ... exploded.

"If only Hugh hadn't written that stupid article." Greg pounded his fist against the steering wheel. "I knew something bad would happen the moment I saw it. And I still wasn't fast enough."

Now *he* wanted to punch Hugh in the face.

Gravel spewed away from his tires as he whipped into the driveway of his small ranch-style house. It wasn't new or anything, but it was his. And he'd been looking forward to having people to share it with him.

The ring between his fisted fingers cut into his skin, but he didn't care. Could he get his money back? He gripped it even harder, relishing the pain. He didn't want to return it to the store, but back on the finger he'd bought it for.

I didn't even pay attention to the return policy the clerk talked about the other day. He shoved the warm metal back into the velvet box and shuffled through the papers on his counter, wondering where the receipt had gotten. There.

"Six months."

Leaning against the counter, arms crossed, he tried to reign in his thoughts. They'd been flying around as if caught in a tornado ever since she dropped the ring next to him. *Think, Greg. Think.*

Could he convince her breaking off the engagement was a mistake in less than six months? It had taken him twenty-five years to get to the point they were now. And where was that? Nowhere.

He wasn't even sure she'd let him be friends anymore. After all, this mess was at least partly his fault. If only he'd stayed out of it. But no. He had to be the fixer. Make things right. Make Michelle happy.

"Obviously, I'm no good at that."

He plopped down on a stool and cradled his head in his hands.

"I need advice, God. I'm lost."

His gaze landed on the newspaper as he opened his eyes once more. It was a crazy idea. Insane, even. But maybe that's the kind of plan he needed right now.

He pulled his laptop over and booted it up. Here goes nothing.

CHAPTER 21

*M*ichelle got to work extra early, hoping to catch Hugh as soon as he arrived. He must have had the same idea because he waited at the conference table in the middle of the room. As she walked through the door, he held up a paper coffee cup.

"I know you don't like the stuff that gets made here, so I picked something up on the way in."

"Even after everything I said yesterday?" Michelle gratefully accepted the drink.

"You were right about most of it. I had no right to print that article. When Aunt Emma asked me to cover the story, I had misgivings, and I should have listened to them. Instead, I followed the advice of an old woman worried about sales, who—let's face it—needs to retire. Honestly, I didn't even write everything that appeared in the paper. Evidently, she decided it needed some juicing up. I just gave the details. She added the emotion."

Michelle opened her mouth to say something, though she wasn't sure what, but he held his hand up.

"That's still no excuse for me not checking with you. Not to mention making sure my aunt didn't edit it. My father and uncle plan to sit her down this week and make sure some things change around here, but that's beside the point. The point is, I'm sorry, Michelle. I should have told Aunt Emma, 'no.'"

Michelle slid into the chair beside his. "And I should have reacted better. If Greg hadn't caught me yesterday, I really would have hit you. I was that mad and never should have come to church in that mood. It kept me from really worshiping God the way I want to. But I lied to myself and decided I could handle it. I need to apologize to you publicly after making such a big deal of everything before class yesterday."

"I won't ask for that. I know this was hard enough for both of us. And don't let me forget that I owe Greg for holding you back," Hugh said with a grin.

"He's a good friend." She nodded.

"Friend?"

"Friend." She waved her hand to show off her naked finger. "Greg's my best friend, and I decided it would be best to keep it that way. I agreed to marry him for the wrong reasons, and I couldn't go through with it."

"I'm sorry it didn't work out." His voice held the tone of genuine sorrow.

"It didn't work out for marriage, but I think it will work out even better this way." Although she would never admit it, she missed the weight of the diamond on her hand.

"Well, if it isn't the front-page cover story." Emma's voice warbled across from the doorway. "Welcome back, Michelle."

"I'll talk to her." Hugh kept his voice quiet so his aunt couldn't hear. Michelle nodded and waved her hello to Emma, not trusting what she might say if she opened her mouth. She would make it through the meeting, and then she'd go on with her day.

≈

DARCY TEXTED MONDAY AFTERNOON.

Want to talk yet?

Nope.

Greg set his phone aside.

He hadn't heard from Michelle, though he hadn't expected to. After all, she was probably working. Assuming she hadn't still been angry at Hugh and gotten fired this morning.

No. Not going to dwell on that. Not his problem. Remember what happened the last time he tried to fix things for her?

He got his heart trampled.

I'm here when you're ready.

Darcy replied.

Just because things were finally going her way, his sister obviously thought she could make his life better too.

That wasn't fair.

Darcy had been through the wringer over the last year. It was wonderful that she'd finally get to be a mom. Yet another reason not to call her. She didn't deserve his rotten mood right now.

Maybe a distraction would help. Email? Social media? Neither sounded enticing, but he opened his browser anyway.

Local Alum Makes It Big with Family Show

Greg scanned the article. His university showcased graduates who'd gone on to do great things. But this time, he knew the person.

Brandon Jones lived in Heber Springs. His cousins starred in a show about a family who loved to hunt, although it was more sitcom than documentary. Greg hadn't realized Brandon was involved in it, though, since Brandon was also a local youth minister.

The article quoted Brandon. "I love working with my family,

helping them show that there's more to guys who love hunting. And above all, helping them show their faith to people who might not hear about God otherwise."

Greg swallowed some jealousy at how much bigger Brandon's outreach must be than his. After all, the souls Greg helped nurture each week were important, too. He hadn't talked to his college buddy since graduation despite them not living far from each other.

"They're always looking for ways to get the Word out," Brandon stated. "Who knows? We're always open to ideas or businesses we can partner with down the road."

Click.

What had Michelle's dad been talking about the other day? Greg hadn't paid much attention because he'd been so focused on Michelle. But hadn't she said something about the factory needing a miracle to stay open here in Cedar Springs? That having a big name to work with them could save the place?

Would a big name like *Huntin' Guys* be considered miracle-worthy?

If he could line this up, it would take another worry from Michelle's shoulders. There he went again. Trying to keep her happy. But it was worth it.

He'd love her forever, no matter what. Now, to prove it. Isn't that what 1 Corinthians 13 meant when it said love was kind, not resentful, and endures all things? Time to practice what he'd been preaching.

DAD'S TEXT Wednesday morning only said to swing by his office as soon as she could. Michelle braced herself for the worst. When she arrived, everything at the factory looked normal.

"Hey, Dad. It was a lot easier to get in today." Michelle knocked on the doorframe of his office. "What was the urgent text about? You said to come right away."

"I wanted you to get the scoop before anyone else." He tossed a pen down and shot her a huge grin.

Michelle perched on one of the chairs and waited.

"We're not selling." Her dad leaned back in his chair and rocked while she processed what he'd just said.

"What? What changed?" She pulled out her notebook and started scribbling.

"You know that goofy show on TV, *Huntin' Guys*? The ones based out of Heber Springs?"

"Yes." What did that have to do with the greeting card factory?

"Turns out that one of the men from that family happens to be a youth minister in the area, and Greg knows him through their areawide events." Her dad pointed at her. "Greg said you mentioned something about the company just needed some big name to do their own greeting card line, and it would save the company. So, he called his friend."

Michelle leaned back, blinked a few times, and swallowed a lump in her throat. She barely remembered saying that to Greg but was pretty sure it was the same day he gave her the ring. And now, guilt crept over. The same guy she hadn't treated like her best friend a few days ago turned out to be a better friend than ever. Even if he'd said all of her ideas turned out badly, this one was right on target.

"They're going to do it, aren't they?"

"I thought you could help me write up a press release." Dad picked up his pen.

The cards they'd already helped *Huntin' Guys* design covered everything from birthdays and anniversaries to Get Well Soon. She wrote down a few of the comic lines to include in her article and took a picture of several in a collage, arranged so the readers couldn't see the total card but could get an idea of what they might be like. For an hour, they worked to make sure the article would say precisely what the company wanted it to say.

This morning, all she'd been able to tell Emma was that she'd have another article on the greeting card factory. She'd had no idea it would be such an exciting one. Everyone would be completely blown away. And why not? She was. She offered up a prayer of thanks as she drove back to the newspaper office.

Everything in her desperately wanted to pick up her phone and call Greg to thank him, but would he even answer? She probably should have listened to Darcy on Sunday and gone back to talk things through, but she hadn't wanted to face him. If only she hadn't left things unfinished. Had she made a complete mess of their relationship? What would she do if she lost her best friend? Her world would have a huge, gaping hole without him.

Hugh stuck his head in her cubicle as she typed up her article. "Got a minute?"

"Sure." She hit *save* and followed him to his desk, where he pointed to his screen. She read the first few lines and then sat down to read the rest of his retraction and apology for the article printed in Sunday's paper. Another weight lifted from her shoulders.

"Thank you." She leaned back.

"It doesn't completely make up for what happened, but maybe it will make it a little better." He shrugged.

"I saw your dad and uncle earlier. I take it things are settled?" She stood so he could have his chair back.

"Emma didn't like what they had to say, but I think she'll accept it in the long run. They want her to share the managing editorship with someone else, preferably one of them. Maybe me. Just another set of eyes to make sure we don't have to write any more retractions."

"Would you want it?" She leaned against the doorway.

"I don't know. I always wanted to be a journalist. Not really editor. I still enjoy going out and getting the scoop on things, not being stuck behind a desk reading what other people have written. I mean, if it were part-time, maybe, but I've got a lot of thinking to do before I'd actually accept such a position."

"Besides, there are others here more qualified." He tapped

his pen against the desk. "Dan, the sportswriter, for one. I know he's getting older and might not enjoy football stands on cold nights anymore."

She nodded. "I didn't mean to turn everything upside down around here."

"Sometimes things need shaken up."

Back at her desk, she contemplated everything that had happened over the last few months. Moving, taking care of Grace, forgiving herself for the guilt that wasn't even hers to carry. And then forgiving the one who'd started all of this. The fear of losing the card factory and the miracle that saved it. Patching up things with Hugh, then blowing up yesterday and having to do it all over again. Being engaged and then not. Life had definitely taken some twists.

Sporadically throughout the rest of the afternoon, she checked her phone for a missed a call or text from Greg. It was weird for them not to share at least one message a day. But her screen remained empty of notifications. He was probably just giving her time. They were still friends, right? Because the thought of a Greg-sized hole in her life was too much to accept.

CHAPTER 22

A few days later, Michelle finished an interview with the local Girl Scout leader about the troop taking a trip down to Savannah, Georgia, where the Girl Scouts began. Michelle planned to write an article about the fundraising and patch-earning the girls had done with a follow-up about what they learned.

Checking her phone, she clicked to listen to her voicemail. "Michelle," Diana's voice came over the line. "Kevin gave me your news—that you were hoping your friend could adopt Grace. I think that's just great, but we've run into a slight snag. You know we searched everywhere for relatives of Leah or John and couldn't find anyone.

"But, it seems Leah has an aunt and cousin up in Missouri. I don't think there will be a problem, but we're exploring it, just to make sure. I'll keep you updated. It seems the cousin heard about the deaths and decided to see if she could get anything out of whatever they left. She didn't expect a child and doesn't want another mouth to feed—her words, not mine. We're contacting the aunt to make sure she feels the same way. Keep your fingers crossed."

Michelle took a deep breath. Just when everything seemed to

be going right, this came up. Who said Satan didn't work in the world today? She bowed her head right there in her car and sent her plea heavenward.

"God, You know how much we love Grace, and You know how much we want her to be Darcy and Phillip's little girl. I thought that's where You were pointing me the other day when they made their announcement. But God, I know if this aunt loves and wants Grace, it may better for her to be with her biological family. Father, help us to accept whatever comes. Please, God, show us what is best for our little girl."

Michelle drove straight to Darcy's house to pray with her. Together, Darcy, Sheila, and Michelle all joined hands to petition their heavenly Father some more. After a quick hug, Michelle headed back to work.

It was time to write her final "Dear Emma" column. She'd picked out a letter last week but needed one more to finish the space. She shuffled through the stack of questions waiting for answers. She tossed several to the side right away. Michelle set aside a couple as "maybes," some of which had made it to that pile but no further for several weeks now.

A new missive caught her attention. It was neatly typed on plain white paper, but it was a little longer than some. She smoothed it out and read it.

Dear Emma,

> *My best friend is also the love of my life. We've been friends forever, but I can't seem to find the words to tell her I love her as more now. She seems to want to keep everything the same as it was when we were kids. Should I just leave it as it is and make sure I can at least keep her friendship, or should I work up the nerve and tell her how I feel? I don't want to lose her.*

> *Sincerely, Wants to Be More than Friends*

In the last few months, she'd never covered a letter like this one. She replaced the rest of the notes on the shelf for the regular girl who'd be back next week. Perhaps Betsy could make something from the "maybe" pile. Michelle wanted to tackle this question but had to think about it.

Her gut instinct was to tell the guy to treasure his friendship, but another part of her argued to urge him to be honest, no matter what. What would other people say about this? Did she know this man? The letter seemed so personal to her.

She did a quick internet search and found a couple of answers, but she needed to do this one by herself. Somehow it struck a chord within her that none of the others had done.

Dear Wants to Be More,

Michelle typed:

Have you hinted at such feelings in the past? Could it be that she doesn't know you feel that way and might feel the same?

She stared at what she'd typed and then deleted all but the greeting. She changed it to:

True friendship requires complete honesty. If you can't be completely honest with each other, you're not really friends. Tell her how you feel. If your relationship is as strong as you think it is, it will survive, even if nothing more comes of it. One thing I know is, you'll never know until you ask.

Sincerely, Emma

~

KEVIN TOUCHED base later that day to let her know he and Diana would drive to Missouri the next day to meet the aunt.

"At least we can find out if there are any more family members out there we need to search out. This came out of the blue. The cousin literally showed up in the attorney's office earlier this week and demanded that he give her any money left when Leah died."

"Wow. Were Leah and John well-to-do?" Michelle chewed on the end of her pen.

"Nah. They were just regular people. Probably left more student loan debt than anything. Their life insurance went into a trust fund for Grace. Other than that, they hadn't lived long enough to accumulate much more than love and memories."

"That's worth more anyway."

"Always," Kevin said. "Hey, I went by the prison and met with Charlie again today."

"How'd that go?" She rifled through a stack of old papers on her desk. "Is he receptive?"

"He wasn't that first day I went. But he seemed a little more open today. I'm not giving up. When I first thought of doing this, it was really for me. Because if I hadn't, I could have let the anger and hatred build up and simmer until it consumed me. I'm not okay with that." He paused. "But now that I've talked with him a couple of times, I can see he needs Jesus more than anything."

"Yes. I'm glad to know you're going down there and studying with him."

"Every soul deserves a chance to know there's an opportunity to be forgiven, and Heaven is for everyone. None of us deserves Heaven, but we all deserve a chance to know we can go there, thanks to Jesus." His voice choked up some as he ended.

"Agreed." She leaned forward and rested an elbow on her desk. "We're praying hard for Charlie as well as the situation with Leah's aunt. Keep us updated, Kevin."

"I sure will. And sometime, you'll have to tell me what changed your mind about adopting Grace."

"Someday, maybe I will." She grinned.

After she hung up, the reality of it all hit her again. The day she changed her mind about Grace, she'd pushed Greg back to where she thought he belonged, but now she wasn't so sure. And she hadn't heard anything from him since then. Had she truly blown it?

~

BY THE TIME Michelle saw Greg on Sunday, they hadn't talked in any form or fashion in a week, not since she'd given him back the ring. He greeted everyone around her as her family left after services. Mom invited him for lunch, and Michelle breathed a sigh of relief when he nodded. But he still didn't look at her.

When everyone sat around her parents' table, Greg sat across from Michelle instead of his usual spot by her. Everyone awkwardly slid over one seat to accommodate the difference. Michelle numbly lowered herself in her seat. Here was her proof. Her life would never be okay again. She'd alienated her best friend forever. The conversation flowed around her, but she didn't pay much attention.

"Michelle."

Mom's sharp tone of voice brought her head up from where she'd been studying the pattern in her peas.

"Did you hear Darcy ask if you'd heard from Diana?"

"No." She put her fork down. "She and Kevin were supposed to go to Missouri this weekend to meet the aunt, but I haven't heard from them. Maybe they're just waiting until tomorrow. Normal business hours and all."

Phillip squeezed Darcy's hand.

"They didn't sound worried about it. I think the aunt is older, and if she's anything like her daughter, she won't want anyone else to take care of." Michelle gave Darcy a weak smile. "Sounded like she already had a houseful."

That answer satisfied everyone enough to move on to other subjects. Michelle finished eating and realized she'd taken extra food so Greg could steal some like always, a habit from years and years of sitting next to each other. What could she do with the extra? She looked across the table, but he avoided her gaze.

No way. She wouldn't let him ignore her. That was just as childish as her tantrum from the week before.

"Please pass this to Greg. I actually got it for him." She handed her plate to Darcy, who sat beside her.

Darcy took it with a gleam in her eye and passed it to Phillip, who set it in front of Greg. Michelle wasn't sure, but she might have seen a corner of Greg's mouth turn up. It was enough to give her hope again.

Michelle pushed back from her spot and turned to her mom. "Can I help you get dessert ready?"

CHAPTER 23

*M*ichelle's phone pinged as she typed up an article late that week. A text from Kevin.

Can I come by sometime today?

A little niggle of fear crept into her head. Would Kevin have to take Grace away and give her to Leah's aunt?

Sure.

She sent the answer back before she could talk herself out of it.

It was almost lunchtime, so they set up a place to meet. Out of habit, Michelle started to text Greg to see if he could join them but remembered that he was still keeping his distance from her. It had almost been two weeks. She'd have to do something soon. She was going through withdrawals. It was next to impossible to concentrate, so she gathered her things and headed to the restaurant early.

When she and Kevin sat across from each other, their food

ordered, he gave her a serious look and then grinned. "I wasn't sure what news I'd have for you today until just a few hours ago."

"Please tell me it's good." She wadded her straw paper into a tiny ball. "Darcy and Phillip can't take much more heartbreak."

"It's good."

Michelle joined him in grinning.

"I was hoping maybe you could take me over to her house so I can drop off paperwork and get the process started. We're free to go ahead with the adoption."

"The aunt didn't want her?"

"The aunt, nor any of her children." He took a big bite of salad. "When we got up there, we learned she had another daughter and a son we hadn't known about. Diana had to meet with each one to get their written agreement to give up their familial rights to Grace. At first, they all seemed to want her, but then when they realized what little money was left after the funeral went to Grace in a trust fund, they decided they just couldn't afford another mouth to feed."

Michelle huffed. "As if that's all she is."

"You and I feel that way, but evidently, these people didn't even know Leah very well because her parents and the aunt had been at odds with each other for years." He took a sip of soda. "I'm still not certain how they even found out about Leah's and John's deaths."

"So, you're for sure letting Grace be Darcy and Phillip's?" She could barely control the shriek of elation that wanted to escape.

"I am. It's the first thing that just feels ... right. Like it was meant to be. I hate saying that because I wish Grace could have grown up with Leah and John, but I think this is the next best thing. Even when you and Greg planned to get married, it still didn't feel right to me—like there was something out there that would be better." He shot her a guilty look. "No offense."

"No. I know what you mean. I kept telling myself we were doing exactly what God wanted us to, but it's like in the story of Joseph in the Bible." She used a French fry to sop up some gravy.

"What they all thought was bad in the beginning turned out for good in the end."

Kevin nodded. "It took me a while to see that, and there are still some days I don't see it clearly, but I know what you're saying."

They chatted some more about Charlie and how soon Darcy and Phillip might be able to have Grace move into their home. She drove over to Darcy's house so Kevin could follow her. Then, she watched with tears of happiness as Kevin told Darcy that Grace was free to be adopted. Darcy wrapped her arms around Kevin in a hug so tight Michelle was afraid he might pass out.

Back at work, Michelle put the finishing touches on an article about the local bee population. It wasn't what she usually focused on, but the research for it had been interesting. She typed the last few words and hit *save*.

Just out of curiosity, she clicked over to see if her old job at the Little Rock paper was still available. Last week, when she'd still been upset about the article covering Charlie's arrest, she'd seen it listed. She scanned down the list of open positions, but it was gone.

"You don't have to do that," Hugh said from behind her.

She twirled her chair around. "What?"

"Don't look so guilty." He leaned nonchalantly against her cubicle doorway. "I just wanted to say you don't have to look for another job. I already did."

"What? Where? When?"

"Actually, it may be your old position—in Little Rock. We'll move permanently after the wedding. But I'll move in the next week or so to get settled before Vanessa joins me in August."

"Why?" Just throw in a *how* and she'd have covered all the standard reporting questions.

"Because there isn't enough room on this paper for two journalists of our caliber." He shrugged. "And because I never really wanted to work here. It was a sure thing when I started looking right out of college. I guess I was too afraid—of my family and my own abilities—to keep searching after this position was offered. So, I took the job and stayed here, where it was safe.

"But now I'm ready to get out there and expand. I know you love this town, but you had a chance to see what was out there and still decided to come back. Maybe one day I'll come back too. Until then, please help keep this paper running for my family."

"I'll do my best. And I do hope you come back one day." She blinked. Deep in her heart, she meant those words. "I think you'll grow into an excellent editor."

They shook hands.

"By the way." Hugh stuck his head back in. "Vanessa wanted to make sure you'd be willing to be our photographer. She was upset when she thought maybe I'd ruined that chance for her with that stupid article."

Michelle leaned her head back and laughed. "Of course. Just have her call me with the details."

❧

"WELL, GRACE." Michelle rocked the little girl to get her ready to go to bed that evening. "We won't get to do this too many more times. Diana confirmed what Kevin said today—you're officially free to be adopted."

She leaned back and stared out the window at the moon. Grace sucked noisily at her bottle. The rocker creaked in rhythm as she moved back and forth. Serenity settled like a blanket around the room.

Grace had slept several nights this last week for about seven hours straight, but some nights randomly woke up at three and stayed awake for hours before dozing off once more. Michelle hoped she'd kept the baby up long enough tonight so they could have a seven-hour stretch.

"That looks peaceful." Mom leaned against the doorway.

"That's the hope. Maybe I can get her down easily tonight."

"If she wakes, I can get up with her."

Michelle ran a finger down the baby's soft cheek. "Not too many more nights, and we can just sleep and let Darcy take care of it."

"Bittersweet." Mom wrapped her arms around her middle. "I was getting used to the idea of having her as a granddaughter."

Michelle smiled down at Grace. "I know. But this will be better for her in the long run. I'm not ready to be a parent."

"You've grown up a lot in the last couple of months, haven't you?" Mom came in and perched on the ottoman at their feet.

"Mm." Michelle nodded. "That's bittersweet too. Maybe I should have stayed in Little Rock. I don't seem to fit here anymore. But Hugh is taking my old job there, so I guess I'm needed here for a while."

"Maybe you just haven't found your spot to fit into again. You came home thinking things would be exactly the same as you left them, and in some ways, they are." Her mom squeezed her knee. "But what you didn't figure on was, you've changed too, and that makes home different, even if everything stayed the way it was when you left."

"I guess I didn't realize how much I'd changed. Maybe too much. I think I've lost my best friend, Mom." Michelle's voice cracked on the last word.

Mom took the now-sleeping baby from Michelle's arms and laid her in the crib. Then, she wrapped Michelle in a hug. They headed to the kitchen for a late-night cup of cocoa.

"As shocked as we all were when you and Greg announced your engagement, we were even more shocked when you called it off so quickly. You two had grown accustomed to the thought of being together forever, and that's a lot to get over. Have you talked to him at all since that day?"

Michelle shook her head. "He's avoiding me. I've texted him a few times, but I get no response. I guess I loused that one up, huh? I never should have said *yes* in the first place. I knew it was for the wrong reasons, but I still decided to do it. Now I've lost the only guy who gets me."

They sat quietly for a few minutes.

"I think I was also intrigued by the thought of not having to figure out who to marry down the road. You know? I wouldn't have to worry about dating or trying to figure out if I'd get along with his family or where we'd spend Christmas or if he was a good Christian. I know all of that about Greg already."

"What qualities are you looking for in a guy besides what you just listed?" Mom leaned back.

"I don't know. I guess he should be fairly good-looking. Does that make me sound shallow?" She gave a half-hearted laugh. "I want someone good with kids, someone who can laugh at my jokes, and stand to eat whatever I cook. Someone who will support my photography and be a shoulder when I need to cry.

"Someone who likes the same things I do so we'll hardly ever fight over what's on television or which movie to see or how to spend a Saturday. And, of course, godly. I definitely need a strong spiritual leader in my life."

Mom shook her head. "And who do you know who meets all those qualities?"

Michelle thought back to how Greg looked as he held Grace for the first time. All the times they'd laughed together over the same jokes, simply shared a look to know what the other was thinking. When she'd gone on dates through the years and ended up having to see a movie she didn't like or eat at a restaurant that didn't serve chicken fingers and wished she could be with Greg instead. Not to mention how great he looked in that tuxedo a few weeks before.

She'd just described *him*.

"What do I do, Mom? I don't love him like that, but he's what I want."

"Love." Mom set down her mug with such force that some of the remaining liquid sloshed out. "Do you even know what true love is? If you're looking for what they get in the movies or books, you won't find anything close to it."

Michelle raised an eyebrow. Well, that was disheartening.

Mom leaned forward and looked her square in the eye. "But if you want *real* love, well, that's the kind of love that gets you through those weeks when there's not enough money to buy groceries. So, you just eat whatever's in the pantry, even if that means boxed macaroni and applesauce as your whole meal. Love is when you take care of your sick spouse even when you came down with the exact same thing and are just as miserable.

"Love means supporting each other through the good times and the bad like Phillip and Darcy are doing. It isn't butterflies and lightning. It's something you can count on. It's trust and support and reliability."

"But don't you and dad have butterflies and lightning sometimes too?" If those weren't important, there wouldn't be so many novels discussing such things, right? "Isn't that at least part of it?"

"Sure. I had butterflies all over when I first met your Dad." Mom squeezed her arm. "But over the years, I've come to appreciate the other kind of love more. It's what keeps those flutters alive."

"What if you think of him more like a brother?"

"Michelle Denise, do you see him that way, or have you just convinced yourself you do? Because it seems to me like you treat Greg and Mark completely differently."

Michelle held her mostly empty mug in both hands. "Greg won't even talk to me now. I can't just go up to him and say, 'I was wrong. Can I have the ring back?' Right?"

"I don't know, Honey. But I do know someone who can help."

Michelle looked up.

"Pray. Pray that God will help you find a way to make up with Greg. And if the subject comes up again, talk to him. If you can't talk to each other, you can't have any kind of relationship, especially not a friendship." Mom kissed her head as she walked by on her way to bed. "Isn't that what you wrote in your 'Dear Emma' article?"

"You knew it was me?" Michelle spun around so quickly she almost fell off her stool.

"I'm your mother. Of course, I knew it was you." She winked.

So much for that staying a secret. At least two people had admitted to figuring it out now. And Michelle had never even breathed a word.

The mugs could wait in the sink for the next day. There were more important things to do tonight. She turned off the light to the kitchen, but the discussion that had taken place there wouldn't go dark so easily.

Back in her room, her mind spun in overlapping circles as she tried to remember everything that had happened between them over the spring. Had there been more there, but she refused to see it? She closed her eyes and sent her confusion Heavenward.

"God, You know all that I've realized tonight. I'm sorry I didn't see it sooner. Please help me make up with Greg. Even if I can't have a marriage with him anymore, can I at least have his friendship back? I miss him so much!"

CHAPTER 24

*M*idmorning Saturday, Greg rang the doorbell. He held the carton of donuts where she wouldn't be able to see anything else through the peephole. The ring in his pocket worked like a pacemaker, speeding his heartbeat up to a rhythm much too fast.

"Greg?" Her voice came out somewhere between a squeal and a whisper, a feat he hadn't even realized was possible.

"Happy birthday." He shifted his stance, and the aroma of steamy coffee had her sniffing appreciatively.

"That's on Monday." She frowned a little. "Not that I'm complaining, but you're early."

He held a finger up as if quoting an official rule book. "Greg and Mickey tradition says that the Saturday before Mickey's birthday is to be the day of celebration each year."

"Since when?" She crossed her arms.

"Since you got a job and sometimes had to work on your birthday." He opened the cardboard lid and held out the temptations so she could have first pick.

She daintily nibbled a blueberry cake donut and led him to the kitchen counter. Her hair was pulled on top of her head in some sort of messy bun, and an old high school T-shirt that might have been Mark's over a faded pair of yoga pants. There were no signs of anyone else around.

"Where is everyone?" He glanced around the island for the baby seat.

"My parents are at a community event where the *Huntin' Guys* are coming in to meet the townspeople. A publicity stunt for the factory but also a way to make it up to the people who've worried for so long about the changes coming." Michelle held up a finger. "I don't have to cover it because it's Hugh's last article before he moves to Little Rock. Darcy has Grace for the day. And I never know where Mark is."

"Nice to see you dressed up for the occasion." He gave her a half-grin.

"How was I supposed to know you were coming today?" She waved half a donut at him. "You haven't spoken one word to me in two weeks!"

He spun around, cringing. "Right. I guess I should just go then. Sorry."

"Greg." Her hand caught his shirt before he could take a step.

He turned back to face her. This was so awkward. She took the box of donuts from him and set them on the counter. He passed her the cardboard cup with her name on it.

After a sip, she muttered something under her breath that sounded like, "Of course, you know exactly how I like my coffee."

Maybe this had been a bad idea.

"Here or back porch?" She pointed her thumb towards the yard.

"You're the birthday girl." He stayed on the other side of the island, unsure how to do this anymore.

She grabbed her cup, and he followed suit, as well as bringing the box. Maybe if they sat in their old familiar spot, it would make it more like old times. Not that he wanted things exactly like they'd always been anymore. It was so much easier to read advice than take it. After she took her side of the swing, he settled into his.

They each munched on a donut and sipped their coffee in silence. He set the swing in motion, and she closed her eyes as a breeze came across the porch. Early June brought with it the heat of summer weather, usually with mosquitoes and an occasional thunderstorm. This morning was still fairly cool, though.

"You heard about Grace?"

Greg nodded, set his cup down on the porch floor.

"It's sort of funny. The first time I referred to you while I was talking to Grace, I called you Uncle Greg." She picked at a seam coming loose on the cushion. "Seems I had it right all along."

He remained quiet, staring out into the back yard.

"Kevin came up Thursday. He wanted to tell Darcy himself. So, we met for lunch, chatted about that and about Charlie."

"You two are getting pretty close, huh?" Greg hated the jealousy that crept out of his voice, but the question escaped before he could stop it.

She shot him a look, a frown marring her forehead. "I probably won't see much of him anymore since Grace is Darcy's. I imagine he'll just visit over there from now on."

They were silent again. This wasn't the way it was supposed to be. After wishing he could talk to her for two weeks, here was his opportunity, but they still weren't communicating. Why had he come? To sit here and stare at her dad's hedges?

"Greg." She leaned forward, pulled her knees up with her chin almost resting on them.

He faced her more fully, but guarded his expression, not ready to let down barriers too much.

She took a deep breath and then seemed to stuff hundreds of words in her exhale. "I'm so sorry I mistreated you. I had no right to just throw your ring at you that way. Especially not in front of everyone. I should have—" She paused, but only a second.\, "I should have taken you aside and talked it through with you. That whole situation was a mess, but I made it worse. Will you please forgive me?"

"I'm trying." His voice was tight.

"I never meant to hurt you." Tears ran down her cheeks, and she swiped them away with the back of her hand.

"Oh, Mickey." He sighed and set her coffee cup aside, then pulled her across the swing until she was tucked under his arm with her head on his chest. It was as if a floodgate had opened, releasing tears she must have been holding back for months.

When she finally sat back, his shirt had a big damp spot, and her face was splotchy. She wiped her cheeks on her sleeves.

"I messed up your shirt." She gently touched the spot, sending a pool of heat out from the area.

He shrugged and swallowed. "It's been used for worse reasons."

"Like what?"

"I don't know." He chuckled, unable to stop. "It just seemed like the thing to say."

She giggled then, and moisture ran down her cheeks for a whole new reason. "Oh, man, it feels good to laugh again. Thank you, by the way." Michelle nudged his arm.

"For?"

"Helping save the card factory. Dad told me about you contacting your friend with *Huntin' Guys*." She shook her head. "You made one of my ideas actually work."

"You know I'd do just about anything for you. But I'm glad my connections could help this work out."

"Last week, I was beginning to think I'd ruined our friendship forever." She tucked her hands under her legs. "Hearing that you were behind that bit of genius gave me hope we could someday work things out."

"I have a confession." Greg fiddled with a fraying thread on the bottom of his shorts. "I came over here today for another reason too."

She pulled her legs up under her and waited, literally on the edge of the seat.

"I've been thinking all week about how to take some advice that was given to me, but I guess there's only one way to take it. I just need to tell the truth." Was he going to do this? To follow the advice of a newspaper article?

Michelle stared at him, her face innocent and unaware. Time to drop the bomb.

"I love you, Michelle Denise Walker."

She lost her balance and tumbled out of the swing. Literally. She sprawled on the porch floor. He knelt next to her, trying to keep her from getting hurt worse as he held the swing back to make sure it didn't hit her in the head.

"You okay?"

She nodded. "Better than okay."

He pulled her up away from the danger of the swing and cupped her face in his hands. "What are you saying?"

"Did you mean it? What you just said?"

"Yes. I've loved you since elementary school. It just about killed me to see you go out with all those other guys growing up. And then I was the one who had to pick up the pieces when they broke up with you." He looked skyward and then met her eyes again. "Do you know how hard that was?"

She shook her head between his hands.

"It was hard." He pressed his forehead against hers.

"So, Hugh was right all along." She blinked. "It seems everyone else in town saw what I couldn't see right in front of me."

What was she talking about? He lifted his brows in question.

"Hugh said that all the other boys couldn't stay with me because all I did was talk about you." She ducked her head, not an easy task with his so close. "He said no one could compete with you for my heart."

"Do I have your heart?"

She started to pull away, but he refused to let her get far.

"Mom and I discussed love the other night. She pointed out that I was looking at love all wrong, that I was only looking at the butterflies and lightning part, not the even better part. The part I already have for you."

Greg's breath let out in a whoosh. "Does that mean you love me, too?"

"Isn't it funny what you don't see when it's right in front of you? Mom asked me to start listing what I would want in a husband, and when I finished, she pointed out I already found someone who met every single one of my qualifications." She poked her finger in his chest. "I could never find anyone else who matches me as well, Greg."

He pulled her to him and held her there. She wrapped her arms around his waist, and her head fit perfectly in the nook of his shoulder. Was he dreaming? Because if he was, he didn't want to wake up.

"Wait a minute." Slowly, he backed up and got down on one knee. "Michelle, will you marry me? This time for the right reasons?" He held out the ring she'd given back to him two weeks before. Was he rushing things? Was this too much too soon, considering what all had happened before? Or would it stick this time?

Please, God, let it stick. Let her say she'll be mine.

She nodded and smiled as he slipped it back on her finger. "I promise to try and do better this time. But I do have a question. What advice were you talking about when you started this conversation?"

He ran his fingers through his hair with a sheepish grin. "Dear Emma."

$\sim$

MICHELLE SAT down on the swing as the truth dawned on her. That last letter she'd answered as "Dear Emma" had come from Greg. The one that seemed so different, had touched her so much. Had a part of her known even then that she'd be here one day?

"What is it?" He tugged at her fingers.

"It was you." She shook her head, gave a little laugh. "I knew that the letter seemed familiar as I was writing the response, but it didn't even cross my mind that it could be you."

"Wait." He blinked. "You're 'Dear Emma'?"

"Until last week." She covered her grin.

He sat down next to her. "I wrote that letter to the person the question was about. How ironic."

They both burst out laughing. It was a small world, indeed. If they'd paid more attention, they could have solved many of their problems without the last two weeks of misery.

"Do you really want to marry me, Greg?" She nudged his arm. "I mean, look what I've already put you through."

He shook his head. "There is no other girl for me. You've always been the only one."

"And you're okay with me marrying you despite the fact that I don't feel butterflies or lightning?"

"I'm going to kiss you now." He took her face in both hands. "Don't run away, okay?"

She tried to nod but couldn't move. Hopefully, he could see in her eyes that it was okay. He leaned forward, slowly, slowly. He searched her face one more time as if to give her another chance to back away. She inched his way, and he took it as the needed invitation.

Ever so gently, he pressed his lips to hers. Her eyes fluttered closed, and her body moved closer to him. He wrapped an arm around her back and deepened the kiss. The world shrank to just the two of them, her tummy whirled with a vortex of new emotions, her breathing sped up.

When he pulled away, he studied her for a moment. "Too much like kissing your brother?"

She shook her head. "You know what?"

"What?"

"Maybe there are some butterflies after all." She put a hand to her stomach.

He chuckled. "Maybe we should try for the lightning?"

And he kissed her again.

How blessed was she? She had her dream job, her dream man, and would get to be an aunt to Grace. And she hadn't even known she wanted the second two items on her list two months before. She sent a silent *thank you* up to God for asking her to participate in saving Grace. Without all of those things happening, she might never have reached this point.

So, in some ways, all this time, Grace had been saving her.

FROM THE AUTHOR

Dear Reader,

I don't always know where a novel will go when I begin it. Oh, I have a general idea, but things don't always end up *exactly* like I thought. When I neared the end of this book, I knew Michelle wasn't going to adopt Grace, despite her burning desire through the story. Just like Michelle, sometimes what we think is God's plan for our life turns out to be completely different, and even better, than what we had imagined.

I hope you enjoyed this friendship-turned-romance story. I love this kind of tale because it's what my husband and I share. Our friendship wasn't over twenty years, like Greg and Michelle's, but we were friends for about half a year before we started dating. And our friendship has only gone stronger during the last sixteen years of marriage, as we grow the kind of love that keeps the flutters alive, as Michelle's mom said.

If you enjoyed this story, I'd love for you to share it with a friend. Also, if you can, please leave a review. Reviews, even short ones, help authors by not only lifting our spirits but also letting others know that people think our story is worth reading. I appreciate it so much.

If you'd like to keep up with me, feel free to check out my website and Facebook author page:

http://abitofanguish.weebly.com

facebook.com/amyanguishauthor

God bless you!
Amy

DISCUSSION QUESTIONS

Questions for Discussion and Thought

1. So many times, we take the verse Romans 8:28 to mean that God will bring good from a bad situation immediately, but it doesn't always work that way. It also doesn't always turn out for the good we expected. In the story, Michelle tries to bring about the good she thought God meant to bring from the wreck, but it turned out differently than she expected. Do you find yourself doing the same thing? What are some ways we can work toward allowing God to bring about what He wants instead?

2. When people think about romantic love, they often think of the emotional aspects. In a relationship, though, you need more than the butterflies and lightning, as Michelle and her mom discuss. Do you think it would have been wise for Michelle to start a relationship without any of the romantic feelings? Or do you think she and Greg could have made their relationship work based on a mutual desire for Michelle to adopt Grace? Did Greg and Michelle have what it takes to make a relationship work at first?

3. Grace's parents desired for her to be brought up in a home with both a daddy and a mommy. Statistics prove that children brought up with both are more stable and better grounded. After all, God created families that way. If you were in Kevin's shoes, would it be easy for you to honor your friends' wishes, or would Michelle have convinced you even before she got engaged?

4. When we go into a situation with our minds set a certain way, it's hard to change them and see what's really there. Michelle has always considered Greg a friend and nothing more, so she doesn't see what everyone else in town does. Have you ever had a situation where you couldn't see the blessings in front of you because of a previous mindset?

5. Even though the town of Cedar Springs hadn't changed much, Michelle had. Have you ever had a time when you tried to go back to the way things were and realized how much you have changed?

6. Greg almost loses his chance to have Michelle as a wife because he's afraid that if he tells her the truth, she'll reject him, and he'll lose her as a friend, too. But as Michelle unknowingly advises him, you'll never know until you ask. Have you been in a situation where you almost lost a chance because you were afraid of rejection?

7. Why was it important for Michelle and Kevin to forgive the drunk driver? Would you have made the same choice in their situation?

8. Michelle's parents didn't think it was a good idea for Michelle to adopt Grace. Did you think they were too supportive or not supportive enough of her desire to take Grace in? Have you ever had someone speak truth into your life that was difficult to hear?

9. If Grace's parents could see how her life panned out, would they be happy with her home? What do you think they would say to Michelle?

10. Do you think the changes at the card company will save the business? Is letter-writing truly a dying past-time?

ABOUT THE AUTHOR

Amy R Anguish grew up a preacher's kid, and in spite of having lived in seven different states that are all south of the Mason Dixon line, she is not a football fan. Currently, she resides in Tennessee with her husband, daughter, and son, and usually a bossy cat or two. Amy has an English degree from Freed-Hardeman University that she intends to use to glorify God, and she wants her stories to show that while Christians face real struggles, it can still work out for good.

Faith and Hope

Hope needs more hope. Faith needs more faith. They both need a whole lot of love.

Two sisters. One summer. Multiple problems.

Younger sister Hope has lost her job, her car, and her boyfriend all in one day. Her well-laid plans for life have gone sideways, as has her hope in God.

Older sister Faith is finally getting her dream-come-true after years of struggles and prayers. But when her mom talks her into letting Hope move in for the summer, will the stress turn her dream into a nightmare? Is her faith in God strong enough to handle everything?

For two sisters who haven't gotten along in years, this summer together could be a disaster, or it could lead them to a closer relationship with each other and God. Can they overcome all life is throwing at them? Or is this going to destroy their relationship for good?

Get your copy here:

https://scrivenings.link/faithandhope

MORE CONTEMPORARY ROMANCE FROM SCRIVENINGS PRESS

Forever Music

A battered heart needs healing.

A community needs rescuing.

A chartered course needs redirecting.

College history instructor, Josie Daniels is good at mothering her three brothers, volunteering in her community, and getting over broken hearts, but meeting aloof, hotshot attorney Ches Windham challenges her nurturing, positive-thinking spirit.

Josie longs to help Ches find his true purpose, but as his hidden talents and true personality emerge. Will she be able to withstand his potent charms, or will she lose her heart in the process?

A rising star in his law firm, Ches Windham is good at keeping secrets.

He's always been the good son, following his father's will to become an attorney and playing the game for a fast track to partnering with a law firm. Lately, though his life's path has lost whatever luster it had—all because of his unlikely, and unacceptable, friendship with Josie. He struggles between the life he's prepared for and the one calling to him now. Opposing his father has never been an option, and spending time with Josie can't be one. The more he's with her, however, the more he wants to be.

When a crisis tarnishes his golden future and secrets are revealed, Ches is forced to reexamine the trajectory of his life. Will he choose the path his father hammered out for him or the path that speaks to his heart?

Get your copy here:

https://scrivenings.link/forevermusic

~

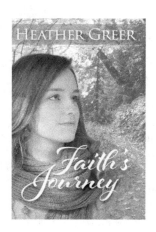

Faith's Journey

Sometimes it's the unexpected path that leads you on your journey back to faith.

Faith's Journey is a contemporary Christian romance due out in February 2018. Set in Carbondale, Illinois, Faith's Journey follows Katie McGowan as she deals with heartbreak, an ailing parent, and her choice between her first love and the possibility of a new love. Through new and unexpected friendships, Katie is challenged to take an honest look at the faith she left behind when she left home and desires a renewal of her relationship with God. In the end, Katie finds the way back to faith and discovers living out God's plan for your life isn't always easy.

Get your copy here:

https://scrivenings.link/faithsjourney

~

Carolina Dream

Sarah Crawford wants more from life than to attend the wedding of her ex-fiancée. An unexpected inheritance in South Carolina comes at the perfect time, just as Sarah is willing to use any excuse to get out of town. When she meets potential business partner Jared Benton and discovers that a house is part of the inheritance, she is sure that God has been preparing her for this time through a recurring dream.

But will a dream about an antebellum mansion, many rooms to be explored, and a man with dark brown eyes give her the confidence to take a leap of faith, leaving friends, family, and her job behind?

Get your copy here:

https://scrivenings.link/carolinadream

~

Scrivenings
PRESS
Quench your thirst for story.
www.ScriveningsPress.com

Stay up-to-date on your favorite books and authors with our free e-newsletters.

ScriveningsPress.com